Love and Mercy - Up
On Roan Mountain

Love and Mercy - Up On Roan Mountain

Blessings!
Martha Arrowood Pelc

MARTHA ARROWOOD PELC

Copyright © 2015 Martha Arrowood Pelc
All rights reserved.

ISBN: 1514279150
ISBN 13: 9781514279151

Dedication

This work is lovingly dedicated to my late father, Steve Arrowood, and to my husband, Russ.

1

The angels are always near to those who are grieving, to whisper to them that their loved ones are safe in the hand of God.

~Eileen Elias Freeman

THE WATER RUSHED down the mountain with a formidable force. The deep winter snow had begun to melt early from the torrential rains of the unusually warm past month. The unrelenting rain had transformed the usually docile, meandering creek into a raging lion of a river, forcing its way into the valley below with a deafening roar.

Ollie had seen it like this only once before in her lifetime. But she was busy thinking of other things this morning. She was cold, for one thing. She absently pulled her thin coat tighter to her chest. She had lost yet another button somehow, and the wind was cutting straight through her slight frame like a shard of glass. She shuddered, but a smile still played across her blue-tinged lips. She had bound her long hair into a bun at the nape of her neck, but a few of her abundant dark curls had sprung loose and fell about her head, framing her handsome face. She was thinking about Tolbert Hensley and his sweet kisses, on this cold morning. He had asked her to marry him just last week, at the church social. He had stammered and tripped over his words until she couldn't help but laugh at him. He was such a sweet boy. She was so happy she felt she might burst wide open. She was fourteen and a half, for goodness' sake, almost an old maid by mountain standards.

"It's about time I was betrothed good and proper," Ollie said to herself.

She felt that just about anything was possible. She would marry and move off to a big city, somewhere far away from the mountain, and wear all sorts of frilly city hats and fancy city shoes. She giggled at her thoughts. She suddenly remembered that Mrs. Hicks was waiting for her, and she quickened her steps. Ollie always helped Mrs. Hicks with her washing on Mondays.

It was not hard work, and Mrs. Hicks paid her a small amount, from week to week, but to a poor girl on the mountain it was a princely sum. It would be money she could use for her wedding preparations. Ollie thought, *I'm all grown up now—well, pert near grown, at fourteen.*

"They surely can't stop us from getting married now." Ollie had easily assumed the role of the eldest child in her family, and with pride. She had helped her mom and dad with the younger ones, as best she could, even at a tender young age. With her mind wandering back to Tolbert, she started to cross over the swollen creek. The water rushing past, under the boards fashioned across the water as a bridge made her dizzy, but she held on tightly to the cut limb that was nailed in place serving as a handrail. The boards of the bridge were slick from the constant moisture. The wood tilted in places, so Ollie stepped carefully.

When she felt the blast of updraft air from the water below, she shuddered again. *It's always so much colder along the creek,* she thought. *Even in warm weather.* She made it across safely and began making her way up the steep stone path that would lead her to Mrs. Hicks's house, hurrying her pace even more.

Suddenly, she heard a shrill scream behind her, back down near the creek. The sound echoed in her ears as it bounced off the gorge. It was a terrified child's scream, and suddenly, it was cut short. Ollie's heart fell.

"Minnie! Ruby!" she cried out in panic. On some days, her little sisters would follow after her and wave their good-byes by the creek. They both were so innocent and loving. Ollie positively doted on each of them as if she were their mother, not their sister.

Surely, with it being this cold, they haven't followed behind me. Ollie's thoughts were beginning to jumble in her growing hysteria. She had warned them not to follow, what with the weather being so bad. Ollie, not hesitating for even a split second, turned back and raced down the path and back to the creek. She saw only a quick flash of color in the frothy water, and then little Ruby's face surfaced. She was gasping for air. Ollie's world tumbled into a spiraling nightmare of panic in that very instant. Ruby and Minnie had fallen into the freezing-cold water and were going downstream fast. Ollie screamed out their names and ran alongside the creek dodging trees and limbs, trying her best to keep up with her two little sisters, but it was no use. Ollie soon realized somewhere deep in her mind that it was futile, but she kept running alongside the creek, sobbing and yelling out for her sisters. Ollie's last glimpse of Ruby was through the trees, just for a moment, and then she was gone.

Two days later, after the water had receded somewhat, they found the girls' tiny bodies about a mile or so down in the gorge, still clasping hands. Their bodies were tangled up in tree limbs, and they hung suspended, like lifeless rag dolls. Their tiny pale faces were a gruesome sight, and one that would haunt poor Ollie for the rest of her life.

Her mother, five months with child, collapsed at the news. The neighbors gathered outside the house to pray, silently holding vigil.

Up in the hidden hollows, tucked way back in these mountains, everyone knew everyone else. It had been that way for countless generations. The mountains somehow just naturally formed isolation. It was isolation like no other. The people on the mountain were all closely joined and any family's event, whether it was joy or tragedy, was intimately shared.

Ollie felt responsible and carried the heavy guilt of not properly watching out for her little sisters, for the rest of her life. Her heart was broken, and she was never the same.

Ruby and Minnie were buried side by side, in the little cemetery that is situated on a knoll, overlooking the tiny valley below.

Etched on the double tablet stone was "Bloomed on Earth, To Blossom in Heaven," with a tiny rosebud carved below each girl's name.

Time danced forward, like a twig floating on the surface of the creek, always meandering, but moving gently forward, on the ever-flowing clear water.

Love and Mercy - Up On Roan Mountain

Illustration by B. Ann Arrowood Williams ~ 2015

2

We all grow up with the weight of history on us. Our ancestors dwell in the attics of our brains as they do in the spiraling chains of knowledge hidden in every cell of our bodies.

~Shirley Abbott

The morning air was clean and sweet, as she stood in the pink-and-golden-hued light. Jane took a deep breath and smiled as its coolness went deep into her lungs. *These mountains really are in my blood,* she thought, as she looked out over the beautiful rolling hills, bathed in color. *Just like my Daddy always told me they were. I feel at peace here.*

Jane knew in her heart that this was where she was supposed to be, and she was glad she had come back home.

Fall always came early to the higher elevations, and the colors of the trees practically rolled down the mountain, in vibrant cascades.

Jane turned back toward the house, and her eyes narrowed as she inspected it. The task before her was daunting. The house was sadly neglected. The eaves were drooping, and thick wisteria vines had completely taken over the first floor.

The house was once proud, almost regal. But now it was squatted, smack-dab in the middle of nowhere, sad and forlorn. Jane remembered the house from her childhood and the happy summers spent here and, of course, all of the family reunions that had been held here. She had seen pictures made in earlier years, and the house before her now was definitely not in the condition it once was.

Sad, but this seems always to be the way with old houses. The decades slide on past and old homes are just left behind, in the overgrowth and tangles of vines, and soon forgotten completely. The family moves away to search for work or just to begin their lives, and they leave the old place behind. The earth slowly reclaims the ground, and all that's left are the hazy memories, lingering in the yard where the home once stood. The memories stay as long as there is someone to remember, and then, those as well tend to blow away with the wind, like dust attached to the scattering leaves.

But not this house. Not my house, she thought, lifting her chin in determination. She didn't realize it, but that same look had once belonged to her dad and his dad before him.

If her dad were still alive, he would have told her that she was "certainly in for it now, girlie," and sure enough, she knew that she was. She felt her dad's spirit right beside her often, and she took great comfort in it.

Even when she had been left practically standing at the altar, she had her father right there, supporting her as always. She could always count on him to talk her through her hardest times. Somehow, he always knew how to say exactly what she needed to hear. She had been twice unceremoniously dumped. Jane thought wryly, *Hey, the day is young, and there's just no telling what tomorrow may hold in store for you, girlie.* She shook her head resignedly. She had never been lucky at love. Not even once. It just didn't seem to be in the cards for her.

One by one, her college girlfriends had happily paired off and gotten married. Starting their families and building their lives, they seemed oblivious to the fact that Jane always stood alone when she attended the weddings. When she was occasionally a bridesmaid, she was all alone, still, in the pictures afterward.

Happily ever after? Really, now. Will there ever be such a thing for me? Yeah, right. She snorted with derision as she shook her head. Here she was, alone again. Standing in the middle of nowhere, looking at the remains of the neglected family inheritance. It was standing, almost in shambles, but her heart, despite it all, still leapt in her chest when she looked at it. "Am I completely crazy or what?" she wondered aloud.

She could almost see the house, fully restored and regal, in all its former glory. Rows of yellow daffodils, happy and smiling, would be nodding their sunny heads in the bright sunshine. And later, the mountain laurel would adorn the front porch with massive dark pink blooms, swaying in the heady perfume-laced mountain breeze, coming straight down off the Roan. Higher, up on the ridges of the Roan, there would be vast rolling fields of pink, with the flowers blooming with abandon.

"Oh, Daddy," she said aloud to the morning air. "There's nothing that I wouldn't give, to have you here with me for this latest adventure." She smiled with a hint of sadness in her eyes. He had been gone a little over a year now, and she was pretty much on her own from here on out. But, her dad had provided her with more than enough spunk to go it alone, and she knew it.

There in the morning light, she could see what was left of the porch would have to be replaced. The main structure looked sound enough, but the porch was pretty much gone. Her mind calculated the cost, and she sighed. "Well, Dad, you sure knew what you were talking about. This is going to be quite a chore. But an Arrowood isn't a quitter." She could hear her dad's words echo in her mind, *Put some gitty-up in your gitty-upper, girlie!* Smiling at the thought, she did just that.

Jane went inside the house, quickly changed into her jeans and a warm jacket, got into her little convertible, and headed back down the mountain. She drove down to the "wide place in the road" that passed as a town.

She had noticed on her way in just the night before, a small diner with a tacky little sign, just blinking away into the darkness. Several bare bulbs were no longer working, and the paint was peeling off some of the lettering. All she could think about was getting started on the house and the sooner, the better.

After winding her way down the slick muddy road back to the blacktop, she breathed a little easier. *These tires are the kind of tires that are supposed to grip mud*, she thought. *Yeah right, they are. Apparently not the serious mud of Tennessee*, she thought with a wry smile. *Maybe that thin flatlander mud, but not this real mucky stuff.* She glanced up at the sign and decided that it had seen better days. *Not the best indicator of what may lie inside.* But, she was feeling just a bit braver than usual on this morning. So she turned into the diner's parking lot, anyway.

"Surely, they have a hot cup of coffee, and something to eat that is at least halfway decent."

After tucking herself into a corner booth in the tiny café, she began to feel better. She held the hot coffee cup with both hands and sipped the bitter brew. She enjoyed the warmth of the steam on her cold nose. It was surprisingly good coffee, after all.

The waitress sauntered around from table to table, filling the coffee cups, with her wide hips swaying to and fro. Jane looked up when she approached, and when she saw her swaying walk, Jane found it hard to look away. But Jane was taught not to stare, and even with hips like that, she was sure the waitress didn't like it when someone made her feel self-conscious about it.

The waitress didn't seem to be that happy in her current job. It was clearly evident by the less than ecstatic expression she wore on her deeply lined face. Jane thought it was a sure bet that this was one lady who took no guff, not from anyone. "So stop gawking at her, and do it now," Jane sternly cautioned herself, muttering under her breath.

As she continued to try not to stare at her swaying hips, Jane noticed a handwritten sign above the large table, near the counter, that read "Liars' Table." The local folks' obvious attempt at humor but it was probably more likely than not, close to the actual truth. The decor of the diner was just terrible, pure eighties pseudo-country. Dusty lace-edged and wooden pink-lettered "Welcome, Friends" signs were hung everywhere, with a smattering of those horrible paintings done on the inevitable black velvet. Jane thought with pursed lips, *Well, if they were shooting for "Trailer Park Tacky", I'd say they pretty much nailed it.*

Jane glanced out the diner's window as she sipped her coffee, and she caught a flutter of movement high above. She tucked her head and leaned in closer to look out and up at the telephone lines. Sure enough, it was prayer meeting time, once again. All lined up was a flock of thirty birds or more, all on the lines. They were sitting side by side, and just chattering away. Her grandmother had always told her that the birds were up there having themselves a special prayer meeting. One bird would invariably be sitting off to itself, a short distance away from the others. That one, her grandmother had always told her with a smile, was for sure, the preacher bird. Jane had always thought that had to be exactly what the birds were doing because her sweet grandma had told her so. She was still pretty sure about it. She took one last glance up at the birds and smiled widely.

As she was topping off Jane's coffee, the waitress looked at her with what seemed like genuine interest. "Are you just here for the day, sweetheart, or are ya spending your vacation here?"

"I'm Jane Arrowood," she said with a friendly smile. "I inherited the old family home place, up the mountain a ways, and I'm hoping to fix it up, and maybe spend my summers here."

The waitress's eyes widened a bit, and she swallowed noticeably as she cast her eyes downward. She slowly lowered the coffee pot until it rested on the table. She appeared to be processing the information as she left an obvious pause in the conversation. The pause, just a few seconds too long, seemed just to hang there, silently in mid-air. Finally she said in a slightly unsteady voice, "Well, my name's Susie and uh, pleased to meet ya, now." Jane could tell she had considered saying more and had decided not to. Casting her eyes away, the waitress pursed her lips with a pensive expression, and quickly headed back to the counter and placed the coffee carafe back onto the burner.

The waitress tapped her pencil on her order book absently and stared off into space, with a blank expression on her face. Then, when the cook rang the bell on the counter sharply three times and barked, "Order up!" the waitress quickly snapped back into the moment and moved fast to grab it.

Jane thought, *That look she gave me was pretty odd*. But she had plenty of other matters to worry about this morning, so she tried just to dismiss it, and she finished drinking her coffee.

Later in the day, when Jane was leaving the store with bulging grocery bags in her arms, she stopped a man heading into the store and asked him where the nearest home improvement store was located. She found it about fifteen miles away, near Elizabethton, just where the elderly man had told her. She bought enough supplies to get started on the necessary repairs.

The main purchase was a kerosene heater to provide some heat, at least until the electricity could be checked out, or possibly rewired. She was sure hoping that a complete rewire job wouldn't be necessary. It was a hopeful thought, but not all that realistic, she supposed.

It's not even full-blown winter yet, she thought. Her first night in the creaky house had been miserably cold. She was afraid of starting a fire in the fireplace before someone made a careful inspection. Her father had always told her the stories, about bats flying into that old chimney and "roosting." *No creepy bats are going to fly into my hair*. She shuddered at the thought. *Not if I can help it, they aren't*. Her lips slipped into an easy grin as she recalled the stories her dad had told her about the bat's reign of terror in the chimney. In the days long gone, the women of her family were all terrified of bats. Dad had laughed about it and said they all had the "stuffing just scared right out of them." It seems that they were all more than just a little superstitious about bats in the house. Regardless of any old superstitions, she wanted no trouble out of them.

Later, when she was finally back at the house, she stood in the "great room," as Dad had called it and looked at the room intently. The rough-hewn log planks still glowed, even in the low light struggling in through the dusty windowpanes of the front porch. There was beautiful old wood here, even if it was in need of a little attention.

This old house is still sound, amazingly sound, Jane thought. She could tell the old logs were the original ones that were part of the old cabin. She felt confident that this was going to work. She could see through the years of dust, grime, and neglect, to the beauty it still possessed. It would be magnificent, once again. She could do most of it herself, and what she couldn't do, she would simply find someone who could. Someone who had the know-how and someone she could trust. *Well, I sure hope I can find that someone*, she thought.

Jane bit her lower lip, pensively. She bowed her head and said a quick, silent prayer and started cleaning. She cleaned everything in the great room, twice, for good measure. The layers of grime were tenacious and required more than just a little elbow grease to buff away.

About a week or so later, she was still hard at work on the cleaning. She carried an old, heavy mirror from the back room down the hall to clean it. The mirror was just beautiful, with an ornate frame that looked like it had been hand carved. The light streaming in from the open front door bounced off the mirror and illuminated the hall momentarily. In the bright flash of light, out of the corner of her eye, she saw a glint. The glint appeared about chest high in the wall, where there was a sizable knothole in the wood. After tearing away layer after layer of old wallpaper, she had finally exposed the old original wooden planks. She sat the mirror down carefully, propping it up against the wall. She examined the knothole closely, and she gingerly poked the tip of her finger in it, to investigate.

Something cold and metallic was on the other side of that plank. "What could it be?" Jane mused.

It was intriguing, to say the least.

Her dad had often hidden things behind loose boards. He had told her of secreted items hidden behind the boards in the house where they had lived, down in the flatlands of the Carolinas. Apparently, this was some old Arrowood tradition. It was that "never trust the banks, when you can bury your money in the yard" kind of thinking. She smiled and slowly shook her head in feigned dismay. "Daddy, what *were* you thinking, now?" Jane chuckled.

Walking back to the bedroom, she searched for some kind of tool. She came back into the hall, armed with a crowbar. As she entered the hall, she suddenly gasped and skidded to a quick stop on the hardwood floor, nearly falling, but she caught herself just in the nick of time. There, in the mirror she had set up against the wall was the reflection of a woman. Dressed in a long black dress with a high neckline, the woman simply stared at her. Jane stared back, frozen in place. With just a faint hint of a smile on her lips, the woman in the mirror beckoned her forward, raising her hand and motioning, and then she was simply gone. When the woman moved, Jane's breath caught in her throat. Then, poof, she had vanished in an instant.

From the angle of the mirror as it sat against the wall, the woman would've had to have been standing in the front room, off to the right. Jane spun around to face the spot, scanning the area where the woman should have been, but there was no one there. She felt the hair on the back of her neck stand up, one by one, and then the hairs on her arms followed suit. *Oh, dear Lord*, Jane thought. *I just saw a ghost, or I have completely lost my marbles, or maybe both.* Taking a deep breath and practically forcing the air into her constricted lungs, she told herself that it was just the sunlight playing tricks on her. She did have a pretty active imagination, after all. *Dad sure told me that enough—like, all my life*, Jane thought.

She was on the verge of total panic, so she tried to keep taking small, even breaths. She steeled her nerves and went to get a coke from the kitchen, talking to herself the whole way. Trying hard to convince herself, she repeated over and over, "That did not just happen."

She leaned at first, and then practically sank against the sink and chugged the drink. *There you go*, she thought, *now your blood-sugar level is getting back to normal. There's no lady in a long dress, no woman with hair gone gray at the temples that once was light sandy brown pulled back severely and matronly, off her face.*

"OK, now. Way too many details to have remembered from a nonexistent glimpse," she told herself sternly. "You have got to get a hold of yourself!"

Taking yet another deep breath, she slowly and deliberately walked back to the hallway, picked up the crowbar, and gently tried to pry the board with the knothole up. She was careful not to look in the direction of the mirror. With her brow knit in determination, she used as little force as possible, trying to be careful not to mar or damage the wood's surface. This wood was precious to her. Her ancestors had hand-hewn these old boards, after all. After a few gentle nudges, the old wood reluctantly let go of the square nail that had held it in place, for at least a hundred years or more.

In the shaft of light that streamed in, the dust swirled around her as the board finally lifted up. *The dust of my people*, she thought with a chuckle. *Now that was a "Daddy thought" if there ever was one. Good, grief!* she thought. *I am such a nutcase! The dust of your people? Really? Why must I always be so overly dramatic?* She rolled her eyes for effect, and instantly she thought with a grin and a nod, *And there you go, again. Dad would have told me that I got all that melodrama from Mom's side of the family, without a doubt.*

She peered into the opening in the wall and could just barely make out the shape of something inside. After a few minutes, with the flashlight now in hand, she aimed the light into the darkness, and she could clearly see what it was. It was an old gun. The gun had to have been placed there quite some time ago, based on the thickness of the dust. Had it not been for the side being mostly dust free, she would never have seen any glint of metal, for sure. The gun was lying with the barrel pointed into the corner of the notch within the wall. She hesitated for a moment, to touch it. Her imagination ran wild with possible scenarios. "Why did someone go to all the trouble of hiding it away, inside the wall?" she wondered aloud, and "When?" Knowing her dad as she did, she figured he knew nothing of it. If he had known it was there, he would have retrieved it for sure.

She hated spiders, so she held her breath, squeezed her eyes shut, and reached in and grabbed the gun. She gingerly pulled it through the planks and out into the light. It was certainly a type of gun that she had never seen before. Not that she had held many guns in her twenty-seven years, but this one was different. It was double-barreled with some metal working evident, even under the layers of old dust.

"Wow, Dad sure would've loved to find this!" Jane exclaimed. The engraving on the cylinder was quite fancy, with intricate scrolls and swirls. She wondered aloud, "Who had owned this gun? What generation placed it behind the wall? When and why?" She just couldn't stop herself from the inevitable flood of questions that tumbled down in her mind. She was her father's daughter, after all. She would just have to find out more about this.

"What juicy past did this gun possess and what would it tell me if it only could?" Jane smiled, thinking about how her dad would have reacted if he had been the one to find it. He probably would have used those very same words, she thought. "Juicy past? Good grief."

She carefully wrapped the gun up in a rag that she had not yet used for cleaning. Then she took it outside and placed it on the seat of her car. She thought about it and then repositioned the barrel so that it was pointing toward the passenger door, safely away from where she would be sitting, in the driver's seat.

Guess I can add extreme paranoia to the list now, she thought with a shake of her head. She went back into the house and continued cleaning the back rooms until the day's light had faded to dusk.

She took some baby wipes she had bought earlier from their package and began wiping some of the grime off her face. She figured that she had wiped at least one layer of dirt off, after a few swipes. This had been a productive day, and she decided that she was going to enjoy the sunset over the Roan, for the first time in years. She was dead tired, but it was a wonderful, good tired.

She marveled that she had begun this adventure and that it was actually going to happen. *Amazing. This house will have life again, life breathed into its very boards, and it will gleam proud, once again.* She smiled in smug satisfaction at the thought.

Moments later, standing on the bluff on the western corner of the yard, still within sight of the house, she was amazed anew at the beauty around her. Her dad had told her endless tales of this beautiful vantage spot. She felt close to him as she gazed at the colors that were on display. Just as quickly as the colors appeared, they softly disappeared. "Oh, Dad, wish you could have seen this with me." She had been blessed to have a dad like hers, and for that, she was thankful.

So, with a tired sigh, her first full day on the mountain faded with the sunlight. She went back inside the house and fell into the little iron bed, exhausted. She didn't even take the time to turn down the bedspread, before sprawling out and instantly she was out like a light.

3

A grandma's heart is a patchwork of love.

~Unknown

I loved their home. Everything smelled older, worn but safe; the food aroma had baked itself into the furniture.

~Susan Strasberg

Jane worked on, for almost two weeks, clearing out the old broken furniture, cabinetry, and such. It was hard work all alone, but still satisfying work. She was not afraid of work, nor was she afraid of getting dirty.

Good thing I'm not afraid of a little dirt, she thought, as she peeled off her bandanna that was stuck, almost glued, to her sweaty forehead.

She had left the gun in the car, still wrapped in the cloth. She decided that she would take it to a local gun shop she had passed, out on the highway about twenty miles out of town.

She cleaned herself up, dressed, and headed back into civilization. She needed to restock her food as well because she had eaten the last bagel this morning, and the small toaster oven she had brought up with her had finally given up.

She found a store in town and loaded the car with the things she needed. The weather was playing on the TV sitting on the counter in the hardware store, and the forecaster warned of a substantial snowfall in a few days' time. She knew, without a doubt, that she wanted to be stocked up, especially when the potential for being snowed in loomed. *This is going to be a test of my physical state as well as my mental*, she thought to herself. She tentatively rolled her shoulder after loading the car and winced. Some of the tearing out of old wallboards had done a number on her muscles, and she needed a bottle of pain reliever and maybe even a heating pad. *Maybe a couple of heating pads*, she thought with a sideways grin.

She had pulled on a stubborn board and had landed square and soundly on her "hind end," as Dad would have said. She had landed with such a fierce thud that it had shaken the whole house.

All this intense labor and she had not even touched the second floor yet. *What was I thinking, attempting a job like this, all alone?* She wondered if it would ultimately prove to be too much. The nightly dreams she had been having were beginning to worry her, quite a bit. They were more like nightmares, she mentally corrected herself. They were beginning to cause her to postpone her bedtime until pure exhaustion had set in, because she so dreaded sleep.

The strange thing was, she had never had dreams quite like this before, and they had begun instantly, her very first night in the house. She even wondered if she could be beginning to dream while she was still awake. It sure seemed to be instant. Her head barely had time to hit the pillow, and the terrors began. She awoke soaked in perspiration, through and through, time after time. Whatever the reason for these horrible dreams, she was ready for them to stop and the sooner they did, the better.

The dark circles that were beginning to form under her blue-green eyes were telling the tale for sure. She hummed a tune that her sweet grandmother had sung her to sleep with countless times, as a child. For a moment, she was transported back in time, to her grandparents' house on Laurel Lane. She drifted back to the smell of chicken and dumplings simmering on the stove and magnolia blossoms floating in a bowl of water on the counter by the sink. *My sweet grandma's wonderful, sunny kitchen.* It was a comforting daydream to which she often returned. The song played over and over again in her head, as it had for the past three days. But things like that had always happened to Jane, from time to time, so it caused no alarm bells to go off. She sometimes knew things long before they happened, and more often than not, smells would accompany the onset of her strange premonitions. They always had. She knew it was her angels.

Softly humming the tune, she pulled her little car into the parking lot of the gun shop. Suddenly, as if on cue, the car filled with the smell of lilacs. It was strong, as if a large bouquet had suddenly been thrust into her face. Lilac was her grandmother's favorite scent. She smiled and said aloud to the car, "Thank you, Grandma, for being here with me. You always know when I need you to be close." She stopped and stared at her reflection in the rearview mirror and slowly smiled. "OK, Janie, you really might be going bonkers, after all," she said to herself. "What's next?" She shook her head lightly from side to side.

"Maybe you need some warm milk and a long night's sleep, girlfriend. Maybe that's exactly what you need." She laughed softly. She noticed movement beside her, and she turned and looked out the window on the driver's side and muttered, "Good grief" without moving her lips. She tried to keep a pleasant smile pasted on her face. There was an alarmed lady clutching her purse tightly to her chest, standing right beside Jane's car, peering down at her with a peculiar look on her face.

Well, all righty now, she thought with an eye roll aimed at the rearview mirror, *I can add talking nonstop to myself to the list of "what not to do in public."* The wide-eyed lady moved quickly away from her car door, still tightly clutching her purse, and cast a nervous glance over her shoulder as she hurried away and inside the store.

Jane could not help but giggle at the sight of the woman peering back, all wide-eyed, with her eyebrows raised comically. *Obviously, I look like a dangerous foreigner in these parts, and someone needs to alert the proper authorities at once*, she thought with a grin. She grabbed her purse and the gun still wrapped up in the bundle and went inside the store.

"Well, one thing's for sure, this here gun is pretty old, Missy," the grizzled and slightly grubby man behind the counter said. He sniffed and when he did, he made the most curious snorting noise. Then his mustache stood out on end as he pursed his lips. He looked like a deranged porcupine, and, stranger still, he looked very much like many of the other locals she had seen around here. He needed a shave badly, and a shower wouldn't hurt anything, either.

Yikes, Jane thought, as she stood looking him over as he hovered, inspecting the gun. Everyone in this area looked like they could use a good scrubbing. Feeling a tad guilty for such a mean-spirited thought, she recalculated. After consideration, she determined that they all just had the look of hardworking folks. And glancing down at her own less-than-perfect appearance, she thought she must have looked like she fit right in as a local girl. She grimaced slightly.

She needed to find a Laundromat and get the oil changed in her own jeans before she went about passing judgment on the local folk's current state of unclean. She had braided her long hair and fastened it with a barrette, but that was all. Her sun-streaked auburn hair was "undoubtedly, your best feature," her dad had always said. "That hair color is the Scotch-Irish in you," he'd say with a grin, "but those dimples now, why they're all mine."

Her mind wandered back in time, for just a moment, and then she popped right back into the present. She tried to focus intently on what the man was saying. Jess, the gun man, cleared his throat, pursed his lips again, and said, "What you got yourself, right here,

Love and Mercy - Up On Roan Mountain

now, is an old LeMat, sure enough." He nodded curtly as if he totally agreed with what he had just said.

"It's a grape-shot revolver," Jess said. "Actually, it's a nine-shot 'n' cap ball revolver, dating from the Civil War. Sixteen-gauge barrel with engraving on the cylinder. Pretty good shape, it looks pretty clean for being this old. It must not've seen all that much action. Where'd you happen to come by this 'un here?" he asked her, smiling at the gun then casting Jane a studying glance, with his eyes narrowing. His brows were as bushy as any she had seen in her whole life. She imagined them suddenly wiggling to life, two thick fat wooly worms perched precariously atop his brow. *Stop that, right now, girl,* she thought as she struggled to choke back a giggle.

"Well, I found it while I was working on an old house," she said after regaining her composure. Honestly, it was as near as she could get to composure after she pinched the fire out of her own thigh. That leg-pinching thing just didn't seem to work as well as it had when she was just a "tadpole," as her grandpa would have said.

She didn't want to offer up too many details to this strange man, and she sure didn't want to give away her exact location. *Who knows,* she thought with another internal giggle, *why, those eyebrows could be loaded and deadly.* She grinned in spite of her leg still throbbing from the pinch. She was up there alone on that mountain ridge, after all.

"I found it hidden in a wall, behind the old original wallboards. Amazing that it dates to the Civil War," Jane said. "Is it common to still find them these days?"

"Well, back in the day, maybe. But it'd be pretty hard to find them these days, I'd imagine." He turned and with much flourish, loudly spat tobacco juice into a metal can that looked like it had been on the counter for a while. And it appeared that he had missed the can more than just once or twice. *Thoroughly disgusting,* Jane thought as she recoiled slightly and wrinkled her nose.

Turning away slightly so that he did not see her face, she mumbled a monotone "Thank you, kindly" to him for the information.

Then she quickly wrapped the gun back up in the cloth and headed for the door.

The man said, "Don't you go, now, and sell it before giving me first chance at it." She nodded quickly in agreement, and the bell on the door tinkled merrily as it closed behind her.

She was glad to be out of there and back outside, in the fresh air. *Whew, that man was a walking advertisement for deodorant and plain old soap!* Jane thought.

4

Well, I don't suppose you have to believe in ghosts to know that we are all haunted, all of us, by things we can see and feel and guess at, and many more things that we can't.

~BETH GUTCHEON

BACK UP AT the house, she carried her groceries inside and put everything away. She went out to the car to bring in the last of the cleaning supplies. Over the top of the trees, a light breeze brought in the clear, cold smell of snow. The old-timers had always said that you really can "smell the snow when it's a-coming." *Well, maybe they were right.* She stood there in the cold air, deep in thought, with her hand still resting on the car door. Then suddenly the distinct sound of a banjo being picked expertly came wafting in, over the trees. With each breeze that blew, the swell of sound seemed to grow louder, and then quickly diminish.

She smiled and imagined an old-timer sitting on his porch, picking a lively tune on his beloved banjo. Each of the notes he played swelled on the breeze and then dwindled, along with the last few moments of daylight.

Sounds as if it's coming from somewhere over in the next holler, she thought. Then she realized that it sounded more like it was coming from over near Winter's Hollow. She loved to hear a lively banjo tune. It did her heart good, always lifting her spirits. She couldn't stop herself from tapping a toe to the beat while beating out the tempo with her fingertips, lightly tapping on her leg.

She continued her work in the house, and in the week that followed, she accomplished quite a bit. The night terrors subsided somewhat, and she wrote them off, for the most part, anyway. It seemed more than reasonable to her that she was just working through her stress. A delayed reaction to the stress she had not fully come to terms with, before. Now, with all the hard work of late, it was flowing out and away. If that was the case, and hard physical work was working, then she was going to go at it even harder. *Full speed ahead,* she thought with heartfelt conviction.

The nightly banjo "hillbilly jamboree" continued, and she braved the slightly colder breezes each evening to stand outside to hear the music that wafted in over the tall pines. It was almost as if the lively music had blown over the trees on its own, making its way straight to her with a definite purpose.

She awoke late one night, completely covered in perspiration. She was breathless and terrified. *What's happening? Where am I?* Jane's thoughts came to her in a fuzzy haze. Then she heard the unmistakable sound of Patsy Cline's crooning, coming from the front room. The scratchy sound of a 45 record with the needle stuck was playing, "I fall to pieces…each time someone speaks your name…I fall to pieces…time only adds to the pain…I fall to pieces."

Who's playing music here at this time of night? Her brain, still half-asleep, formed the thought with fuzz stuck around it. Then it suddenly dawned with clarity where she was, and that there was no one else here with her. She reached over and picked up a short piece of molding. It had been standing in the corner, by the dresser, and with it in hand, she made her way out into the hallway. The molding was flimsy protection, but it was all she had handy. *Even a bendable "eye gouger" is better than nothing at all*, she thought.

Keeping her back close to the wall, she padded softly in bare feet and made her way to the sound of the music. Then, standing there with her molding in her hand, held like a weapon poised to strike, she realized just how dangerous it was, to be out here in the middle of nowhere, all alone. *Well, it's a tad too late for that revelation, you silly girl*, she thought. She pounced into the great room with all the feigned fierceness she could muster and let out a feral cry, with her heart thudding like thunder in her chest. There sat the record player on the end table by the sofa, with the record spinning in the empty room. Patsy's lilting voice sang her lament, over and over. How the record player got turned on was anyone's guess. Her mind raced as her eyes darted all around the room. *Well, maybe I'm sleepwalking again*, she thought. That had to be the only plausible explanation here. The record player was old. She had found it in the walk-in closet in the large downstairs bedroom. It had a canvas type "case," of sorts, in an old army-green color. Still covered in dust, with no fingerprints in that dust, and somehow, it was plugged into the wall. *Simply amazing, that I did this in my sleep, and somehow managed to get the old thing playing, as well.*

She hadn't walked in her sleep in years, but she had managed some pretty remarkable feats in her past episodes. *What's up with this, anyway?* Jane thought. She remembered that her sister had once unlocked her bicycle and started to take a midnight ride, while she was still fast asleep. She knew that stranger things had happened in her family, and this had to be the explanation. Well, it was the only explanation that she would allow her mind to accept, for now.

Strange new surroundings, meeting strange people, having totally new experiences—there's no telling what that can do to someone, mentally.

She took a deep breath and allowed her heart rate to slow. *It has to be sleepwalking*, she thought with a ragged breath. *That's definitely what this is, just another strange sleepwalking episode.*

She made sure she had carefully unplugged the record player. Jane took the cord and wound it up securely around the holder on the back of the player. Then, on second thought, she carefully tucked the end of the cord tightly within the coiled wire.

After looking pointedly at the unplugged cord twice, just to be sure, she padded back to bed.

Soon she was safely back under the covers, and the unplugged record player was sitting in the shadowy front room, on the table where she had left it. The record player switch suddenly clicked off, all by itself. But Jane never heard the small click at all.

She woke in the morning light to the sound of someone reciting what seemed to be a poem. "You cannot hide from the past. The truth must be set free. Remember the innocent who died, hanging from that tree." A woman's voice softly repeated the phrase until the sound became a faint whisper. Jane kept her eyes closed, listening, half-afraid to open them, terrified of what she might see. "Some things are better not seen, and this can't be good," she reasoned. "I know I'm awake," she said to herself. "I'm awake, so this is not good. This is extremely not good."

So, after letting a few more moments pass, she opened just one eye. Nothing was there. "Thank goodness!" she breathed. The blasted record player was not playing, either, so she sank back into the pillow with relief. "Remember the innocent." Is that what she had heard? She wasn't positive, but that is what it sure sounded like to her.

Her grandmother had told her all about the strange and sometimes scary tales of the family since she was just a little girl. And her aunts had picked up the tradition and filled her head up with nonsense, as well. They meant no harm, and she had to admit it was quite entertaining. But it was no wonder that when she came up here in the middle of nowhere by herself, her mind began playing silly tricks. It was just something that occasionally happens. They meant well, but enough of that scary stuff was told to her in her growing years, to cause permanent "dain brammage." Jane giggled at her thoughts.

Those sweet Aunt's of mine, they sure do know how to have fun. Most girls tended to giggle and cut up, but when you put at least two of those Arrowood girls together, now they are something else, always have been. *You know it's really bad when you do such crazy things that you crack yourself up*, Jane thought with a sideways grin. After thinking about it for a moment, Jane laughed out loud. "Well, surely with the family I have, insanity was inevitable." Jane sighed.

What can you do about it now? she thought reasonably. *Not one single, solitary thing, girlie.*

She tried to push the record player incident to the back of her mind, along with the lady's reflection in the mirror. "Some things just don't need to be addressed when you are up in the dark woods alone, and miles from civilization, right?" Jane muttered to herself. She nodded in total agreement.

She got the creeps just looking at the record player, at first, but she soon cured that by playing the Patsy Cline record over and over. She put the record on and sang along, just belting it out as she worked, and it seemed to keep her mind busy, at least for a while.

She thought about her family and how much they truly meant to her. Crazy and funny may run in the family but life is short, and you just have to love them no matter what. I'm going to love them for who they are and what they are. *Life is way too short to focus on just the bad or the sadness*, she reasoned. *Laughing never hurt anyone and maybe even helped some. We have had more than our share of sad times. If laughter really does heal, then our family tree is chock-full of healthy, robust nuts*, she thought, grinning.

With a smile on her face and still lost in her thoughts, she used a screwdriver to pry up a bent nail in the window casing. When the tip of the screwdriver jammed into the wood and slid past the nail and off the casing, the force of it rammed the screwdriver tip nearly an inch into her forearm.

She screamed out in pain. Jane was disgusted with her own lack of attention. She simply had not been watching what she was doing. "Now, why did you go and do that dumb thing?" she admonished herself. She grabbed at the wound, putting pressure on it to try and stop the blood that was flowing down her arm. The pain was intense and tears filled her eyes. She ran to the kitchen table and scrambled one-handed through the piled up stuff until she found her medicine kit. She was able to slow down the bleeding, for the most part, after applying pressure for a while. Then she bandaged the arm as best she could with one hand. "OK, I have done more than enough damage for one day," she said aloud.

She made herself some supper. Using one arm was tough, so she decided on something easy. She had brought up six quart jars of canned vegetable soup from home. Jane thought, *Well now, if ever I deserved good homegrown tomato soup, tonight is the night. It's delicious, even if I did make it myself.* She smiled at the thought. She grew her little vegetable garden every year, just like her dad had taught her. She had dropped seeds behind her dad's plow from the time she was old enough to walk. She'd been taught to love growing things. *A garden patch would be nice here, too, in time.* In fact, she had already picked out the perfect spot of ground.

She had yet another fitful night's sleep and woke bleary-eyed the next morning. Moving her arm under the pillow, she winced from the soreness. Instantly, she remembered the screwdriver incident. *Wow, but that still smarts,* Jane thought as she yawned out loud with a stretch.

She yawned once again, and lifted her arm closer to her face and tried to focus her sleepy eyes on it. Red and angry looking, the wound didn't look good, not at all. All around the perimeter of the wound she could feel the heat. That meant infection.

She remembered her dream. It floated into her thoughts like a cloud and then she suddenly thought to herself, *I need rattlesnake weed—better still, some plantain. Whiteman's foot.* She stopped short as she was starting to get out of the bed. "White man's what?" she said aloud. "Now, where in the world did that come from?"

Thinking she must still be asleep, she threw back the quilt and pulled on her jeans, and went to wash her face. *I need to get some meds for my arm*, she thought absently. She pulled on her hiking boots, not truly knowing why, and made her way out into the cold morning sunshine.

She had seen what looked like an old trail that led into the woods at the edge of the backyard. She tromped through the brown grass and over to it. After a short hike up the trail, she knew she had found what she had set out for, but had not a clue as to why.

"How do I know about this?" Jane wondered aloud. "I don't know how I know, but this weed is a healing plant and making a spit poultice will help my infected arm," she said to the trees that surrounded her. She knelt down on one knee, in the cold frost of the morning. The moss was thick at the base of the pine, and she pulled up the broad-leafed plant, roots and all. She tucked it carefully into her pocket. Back at the house, she washed the leaves of the plant, and then slowly chewed them until they moistened into a clump. She spat it out into her palm and placed the wet clump directly onto her wound and rolled gauze around her arm, to secure it in place.

Later that evening she removed the wrap, and the redness and heat had subsided. She chewed more of the plant for a new poultice and rewrapped the arm. *Amazing what you can just suddenly remember, out of the blue. Some small bit of knowledge that you somehow just absently file away after reading it or hearing it, sometime or another, and then you up and pull it right out of the air. It's just amazing*, Jane thought to herself. The fact that she had dreamed about the plant and had been given instructions on how to use it was totally forgotten in the bright light of day.

That night, in her restless dreams, the lady in the mirror told her of another remedy to help heal her arm. Again, come morning, Jane did not remember that the knowledge had come from her dreams. It was what the lady thought best—better to not overwhelm Jane all at once.

The medicinal plant she had sent Jane into the woods to search for was one of strong power, but gentle healing. It was soothing to Sarah Ellender to be able to help her family once again, just as she had done in the old days. As she always had, Sarah Ellender felt a deep sense of pride, in being able to help. As Jane fell asleep, she whispered absently to herself to remember to "Thank the sweet lady in the mirror."

The people who lived on the meadows and in the valleys of the Roan had relied upon its bounty for centuries. It supplied them with shelter, food, and an ample supply of medicinal plants and herbs. The settlers learned in a short time what the Roan had to offer, as had the natives before them. The mountain folk knew the plant well that Jane had gotten from the woods. The plant, along with many others, had slowly found its way across America following the footsteps of the early settlers. That is how it came to be known as "white man's foot." But Jane had no way of knowing this.

Jane's arm healed up quite nicely. As she looked at the scar where the puncture had been, she marveled that it had healed so quickly. Jane felt a sense of connection with the past. She had returned to her roots and relied on the land, just as her people had done before her. Her dad had told her many times that the Roan supplied your needs if you just knew where to look. There were so many aspects of the Roan that simply awed Jane. It was a magical place, no doubt. Its flora and fauna were nothing short of amazing. She felt that this place was surely "God's country," just as her dad had always told her.

The music that wafted down from high atop the Roan continued almost every night, and she was almost sure she heard a full orchestra of mountain musicians, playing now. The music would swell in the breeze and bring beautiful melodies that fell on her ears, like soft pine needles falling to the forest floor below. The music was every bit as beautiful to her as the fragrant pine needles smell, when the air on the mountain is so cold, you can see your breath in frosty plumes before your face. No artificial air freshener could ever compare to how wonderful a forest of pines in cold wintertime smelled. *If only I could figure out how to bottle that stuff up, I could sell a million bottles*, Jane thought.

One day she would find the source of that beautifully haunting music and dance to it, she promised herself. Jane thought, *There must be a dance hall somewhere nearby, and I am going to find it.*

Over the treetops, music wafted slightly louder this evening. It was old music, from another time and place, and as it was carried on the air, high above the mountain, the mountain itself seemed to sigh.

Once, years and years ago, the band played nightly at the Cloudland Hotel and on clear, cold nights the long-gone band could be heard, playing still.

Off in the distance, a train whistle blew a lonesome sound, out into the clear, still night air. It was not quite loud enough for Jane to hear, and she did not know that a train was once heard rumbling up the old mountain. Long ago, the train whose whistle sounded had carried those looking for rest, up among the clouds. It carried those who were traveling up for a night's stay or a week's vacation in the mountain air, along with all the supplies needed, at the fashionable Cloudland Hotel.

Others had heard the whistle through the years, down below in the village. Occasionally, it still was heard, and strange puffs of steam had been seen rising along the ridge along the train's old route. But these types of things were seldom discussed. Some things are just better left alone, and not voiced aloud. Things such as these are better left to be pondered and sorted out in your own mind. Many did just that, each coming to their own conclusions. Strange happenings like this were common on the ancient ground near the Roan.

The change in the house was remarkable. Just elbow grease and a few replaced pieces of molding had worked minor miracles, it seemed. Time, ticking away, seems to have a way of draining the life right out of a house when no one lives there. The earth soon starts to claim it, and quickly there is widespread disrepair.

Every nail that Jane replaced and every swipe she made with a cleaning rag was filled with love. It was as if she was bringing back that life that had gone away over time. Jane knew that the homey quality of the house was slowly returning, and it was beginning to feel like it was honestly hers.

As winter began to settle in, there was another light dusting of snow as if Mother Nature herself wanted to add it, just for effect. It looked as if powdered sugar had been sprinkled generously over the treetops. Jane knuckled down and continued her repairs.

The locals of the Roan area called themselves "villagers," with the area just below the Roan being the "village." They had truly welcomed her arrival over time, and some drove up occasionally, to check on her and the progress with the house. She was finally fitting in and was being accepted. It sure felt good.

Christmastime finally rolled around, and she planned on going back to Gastonia, to spend time with her family. As Jane drove through the tiny town, hands were thrown up in greeting. Many smiles and friendly nods were offered, as she went past. She felt a tinge of sadness leaving her home on the mountain. It was becoming hers now, and she felt very protective of it. She felt really good about what she had accomplished. Each and every step brought the house closer to what it once was.

Back in the flatlands of North Carolina, she somehow felt instantly out of place.

5

Time is too slow for those who wait, too swift for those who fear, too long for those who grieve, too short for those who rejoice, but for those who love, time is eternity.

~Henry Van Dyke

"Well, hey there, sweetheart. So glad to have you finally back home," Aunt Hilda said excitedly when Jane walked through the front door. Hilda grabbed her up in a big hug.

Then, Aunt Ann hugged her tight, and said, "Guess there are no 'tell-e-o-phones' up there in 'them there' hills these days?"

Jane laughed. "No, there really isn't, Ann. To tell you the truth, I have to travel miles to get even a decent cell signal, and then I have to hold my leg out to help with the reception." Jane giggled. "They really do pipe in the sunshine up there on that mountain. The only way I can get Internet service is with a satellite signal. I'm serious about that, now, no kidding." Jane raised her eyebrows for effect.

Aunt Ann grinned and hugged Jane again. "My goodness, girl, but we have missed our Janie."

"Have you lost weight?" Aunt Hilda said. "You sure look thinner."

Jane smiled at her two sweet aunts as she shook her head in feigned dismay at the bogus weight-loss comment. She slid an arm around each aunt's waist and pulled them to her. They were sure sweet fibbers, big-time, and Jane well knew it. She said, "I have missed you two, so much."

The house smelled absolutely wonderful. They had already gotten started on the Christmas goodies. The day was spent baking, cooking, eating, and swapping stories. The sisters could tell some tales, and time spent with them was never boring, that was for sure.

After a few pies had been made and left to cool on the counter, Jane began telling them about the house and the progress she had made so far. But the story of the self-playing record player and the gun with the possible sinister past hidden away in the wall, were both left for another time. Jane did not want to upset anyone at this festive time of the year, and besides, no harm had come to her. Jane surely didn't want to hear any flak about her having an overactive imagination, either.

Jane didn't want to be accused of making a "mountain out of a molehill" until she at least had all the facts at her disposal. Maybe they would even tell her that they thought she needed to "talk to someone, sugar"—in other words, see a shrink. So, she resolved that she would not talk of any of the unexplained activity in the house, not right here at Christmastime, especially. Christmas was a special time in her family, and she sure didn't want to spoil it for them.

Aunt Ann and Aunt Hilda were sisters of her dad, and she loved them both, dearly, just as her father had. Just putting more than one of these siblings together in a room was sure to bring on side-splitting laughter to the point of tears. Both sisters shared a deep love of family, and both had the winsome good looks that ran in their family line. High cheekbones and broad, genuine smiles were certainly prevalent in this family. These two knew how to have fun and enjoy life.

Aunt Ann leaned in and peered closely at Jane when she reached in to get the cookies out of the oven, and she noticed the still quite evident injury, to Jane's arm. It was healing, but she still saw it. "So, Missy, where'd you get that big ol' gash?" Ann demanded. Jane said that it was just a scratch that came with the territory, when you were working on an old house. "Scratch?" Ann said emphatically. "That doesn't look like a scratch to me, at all. Now that was serious, Jane."

Jane ran her fingertip along the scar. She thought again about the hike into the woods to retrieve the nearly frozen weed, roots and all.

"Ann, what can you tell me about any old medicinal herbs that the family used up in the mountains? Can you remember anything in particular, they may have used?" Jane asked.

Ann stared into space, lost in thought for a moment, and then she raised a finger and announced, "I remember!" Ann was a delightful soul, and she was a pretty smart cookie, as was Hilda Fay. These sisters were quite savvy in lots of different ways. Jane knew she would have to play it cool, or else they would soon suspect she was holding out on the "rest of the story."

Jane kept her gaze averted from Ann's sharp eyes. She cleared her throat to make it seem as if she was not really that interested, but secretly, she was hanging on every word. The two ladies exchanged wondering glances, but Jane's lowered eyes never saw it.

Aunt Ann told the story of their great-grandmother, Sarah Ellender Winters Arrowood, and how she was a midwife in the shadow of the Roan. "Now, Sarah Ellender was born to William "Billy" Winters and Eliza Shell. She lived right on the Doll Flats, at the ridge of the Roan, very near where the old home place now stands. Sarah Ellender was, of course, your second great-grandmother." "She used all sorts of natural remedies to heal the sick."

Ann appeared to be lost deep in her thoughts and did not seem to notice how intensely Jane was listening. Jane went to the sink and washed up a few bowls left on the counter. She dried her hands and carefully folded up the towel and then she reached for a warm sugar cookie and nibbled away at it, with deliberately averted eyes.

"Sarah Ellender was one of the angels born in that family. There were seven girls, and seven boys and not all those girls were good, now mind you. They had seven devils in that brood, for sure. Sadly, a few children did not live long. But the ones that did, now they were sure something else. Mean as the dickens, I tell you. They were so bad that the stories the locals kept alive, with countless retellings, caused those two city fellows who came into the area in the sixties to name that ski resort after them. The little town is now called Seven Devils. And the 'devils' were your very own kinfolk, like it or not," Aunt Ann said, chuckling. "Back then, why, they were nearly famous. Not only were the kids in that bunch ornery, but the story also has it that the father of the brood was every bit as mean as those kids were."

"They homesteaded right up there near where the house stands. They called it the Doll Flats. Never did know exactly why they called it that, but it was pretty famous, up in those parts. People came from far and wide to see the fights."

"Fights?" Jane asked. "What kind of fights?"

"Well, they were sort of what you would call brawls or 'knock-down-drag-out' kind of fights," Ann said. "They were prearranged, organized, and everything. The boys in that family would have "tough man contest" fights to see who was the meanest and the toughest. Likely as not, the Winters clan would win. The daddy, Billy, started the whole thing. That family was terrible mean, by most accounts. The stories that went around told that some were even killed by being beaten with slats of wood, taken right out of the fencing that surrounded the home place. They used just whatever weapon they could get their hands on." Jane's eyebrows went up, and she looked at Ann with wide eyes.

"Some of them are buried right there at the Morgan Branch Church Cemetery. Of course, it used to be called the Richardson

Cemetery, years ago. Well, part of it still is, you know, because of feuding amongst the families up there, a feud that started a long time ago." Ann clucked her tongue.

"When Billy asked for Eliza Shell's hand in marriage, why, her side of the family was not at all happy about it. You really can't blame them. William had built himself up quite a reputation as a hellion, even at a young age, and, of course, he only got worse as time went on."

Hilda added, "Daniel Shell's family were all descendants of Johann Schell, the first settler there, and they were quite a prolific clan. The Shell Creek area Shells were mostly all descendants of this same family.

"Eliza, according to the stories that have been passed down, was left alone, a lot of the time with all those kids to feed. Meanwhile, Billy Winters ran around the countryside kicking up his heels and challenging just about everyone he met to fight. It took him a while to settle down. He was a rake and a rambling man, just like the old song said."

Hilda smiled and shook her head. "I bet that Eliza was sure one that could take care of herself or she wouldn't have married that ol' devil."

"Devil? Why, Hilda Fay, now, that's your ancestor you are talking bad about," Ann said and laughed.

Hilda chuckled. "Well, I am gonna call 'em like I see 'em. Why, I always have, haven't I? There's no use sugarcoating anything now." All three nodded their heads in unison, smiling in agreement.

Ann continued, "Sarah Ellender was a real smart lady. She was left widowed pretty young when Samuel died. She did just whatever she had to do to keep the wolf from the door. Early on, she learned how to midwife. She traveled around helping the local women give birth, and she nursed the sick with her knowledge of medicinal plants. She was paid any old way those poor mountain people could afford to pay her. Sometimes it was a few dollars, but more often than not, it was a bag of potatoes or a sack of onions."

Hilda said, "It was whatever they had, and anything that they could afford to part with. Those poor mountain folks bartered out of necessity. They did what they did to survive, plain and simple."

"The *Pigeon Roost News* would help you to understand what living up there was really like," Ann said. "Harvey Miller was related to us by marriage, and he wrote about the area's day-to-day life and goings on in the local newspaper. Sarah Ellender was taught to use what she had on hand. She was taught how to use the wild plants and herbs that were plentiful up on the mountain since she was just a young thing. She had a working knowledge of how to treat just about any old ailment. Her grandmother Polly Shell taught her everything she knew. There was no money for a doctor when the children got sick. Not many doctors around, even. Mountain people just healed themselves. They used the land for everything, just about, and relied upon it to provide what was needed."

"God provided it, sister," Hilda added with conviction. Ann nodded in agreement. They were right, of course. God had provided the Roan and all facets of its natural bounty to the people who had little else, besides the land on which they lived.

Jane wondered about Sarah Ellen. Could she be the one that was trying to help her? Was that even possible? *That's nuts*, she thought. She shook her head from side to side, trying to come to terms with her thoughts. "That can't be what you are honestly thinking now, girlie. Now, that's just pure nuts," Jane muttered quietly to herself, just out of earshot of Ann and Hilda.

Ann continued with more on the subject, later in the day. It was not easy to stop her once she started telling something interesting. But it was not easy to stop any Arrowood, for that matter. Aunt Ann clapped her hands together suddenly, as she was beginning another tale and exclaimed, "I haven't even put my chopped cherries into the batter yet! I have actually discombobulated my own self, somehow. Oh, Hilda Fay, are you going to let me rattle on and forget to add those wonderful cherries? Now, what kind of fruitcake would it be, without the cherries?"

At the sharp sound of Ann's hands clapping together, Jane was startled and accidentally dropped the last chunk of warm cookie she had just started to pop into her mouth. With wide eyes, she spun around and grabbed the container of cherries and practically thrust them at Ann.

Hilda laughed out loud at Jane's wide-eyed expression and calmly said, "Ann, absolutely no one can stop me when I get wound up talking, and no one is gonna stop you, either." She grinned widely and said, "I have got only one word for you, and its "Maudacious." Ann grinned and then all three erupted into bubbles of laughter, and Jane held her cookie in her mouth as best she could without choking or spewing. Either one was likely, laughing as hard as she was.

"Maudacious" was the family term that meant anything that was over the top and totally "Maudie." Maude Arrowood was the mother of Ann and Hilda and the precious grandmother of Jane.

Maude was truly a one-of-a-kind lady. She made Christmas very special for the whole family. She strung holly decorations on anything and everything, making the house extra festive. Her deep love of the Lord was evident in everything she did. She reached out and touched many lives with her special love during her lifetime. She decorated and celebrated in the unique, truly special way that only Maude could. The term "Maudie" had quickly become the go-to phrase within the family. You could "Maudie" just about anything up, by adding something extra special to something plain, and everyone knew instantly what that phrase meant.

I guess every family has a Maudie of their own, and if they don't, well God bless them, real good, Jane thought with a smile. "They just don't have a clue about what they have missed out on."

Ann smiled and said, "You do remember the 'Maudie Fruitcake' don't you, Janie girl?" Jane had heard the story, of course, countless times, but she couldn't resist the chance to hear Ann tell it once again.

Ann mixed in the cherries and poured the fruitcake batter into the pan and placed it into the piping-hot oven. Turning around to face Jane, she wiped her hands on her apron and slowly smiled.

"Well, Momma was busy cooking for Christmas, and she had invited some of her church folks over to the house to eat," Ann said. "She wanted it to be extra special, of course, what with the church members coming and all. So, she decided to make a fruitcake. She hadn't been married very long, and she was still pretty young. She was still a novice when it came to cooking, but she thought she probably knew enough to pull it off. When she went to mixing up the fruitcake, she knew that some recipes she had read called for some sort of liquor. Having none, she remembered that your Grandpa had a bottle of whiskey, for medicinal purposes, of course, hid out in the garage behind some crates." Ann paused to grin and wink at Jane. "Grandpa didn't know, of course, that Momma had seen him hide that bottle, but she knew exactly where to find it. She poured quite a bit of that whiskey into that cake batter with the intention of adding some flavor. Then she realized that most fruitcakes had a hole in the center of the round cake. The cake just didn't look quite right without that center hole, so she did her 'Maudie' thing, and she improvised, sweetheart." Ann paused, took a small sip of her coffee, and then smiled widely.

"Momma took a can of peas out from the cabinet. She carefully peeled off the label, and she washed that can really well. Then she placed the can of peas directly in the center of the pan with the cake batter surrounding it and put it into the oven. Well, of course, now, the heat from the hot oven caused that can to explode. It sent pea hulls spewing and cascading all over the top of the cake, and, of course, all over the inside of the oven, too. It was a terrible mess."

"When she took the cake out of the oven, she calmly determined that the peas were ok, as they resembled the dried green fruit in the fruitcake. Well now, she wanted to be sure the cake kept good and moist until her guests were served, so she sliced apples and laid them around the cake and covered it up tightly. Later on, Grandpa came behind her while the cake was still cooling and uncovered it to take a peek. Wanting, also, to keep the cake moist, the way he liked it, he poured an ample amount of his whiskey over the cake and let the cake absorb it all in. Satisfied that the whiskey would keep it moist, he covered it back, carefully, and put his hidden bottle back into its hiding place."

"Later, when the guests arrived, the church members, along with the minister, enjoyed the meal that Momma had prepared. After the minister ate two large slices of that cake and was eyeing the platter for a third, your Grandpa took Momma's elbow and pulled her in close. Grandpa whispered quietly in her ear to go easy serving that cake to the minister because she was just about to get him drunk."

They laughed heartily and remembered the many other funny things that Maudie had done. After the laughter had subsided, Ann smiled with tears in her eyes and said, "My Momma was a precious woman. We all miss her so much." "Yes, we do miss her so, every day," said Hilda, as she placed an arm around Ann's shoulders. Jane said, "There will surely never be another Maudie."

Then they all hugged, wiped their tears and then giggled again as they thought about Grandma's fruitcake, just as they had done for many years, and would for many more years to come. The "Maudacious Fruitcake" tale was certainly everyone's favorite.

Later, Ann smiled as she sliced into her own delicious fruitcake, tasted a bite, and then deemed it "Maudie" enough for the rest of them.

"Our precious Maude and Pat did the best they could to raise their family right, in those tough early years of the depression," Hilda said soberly. "They taught us the Bible, and they took us to church regularly."

"They were good parents to us kids, and we were surely blessed," Ann said.

Jane smiled, looking at Ann and Hilda, and thought to herself, *Well, they did an awesome job raising these two, and that's for sure.*

Jane asked if they had happened to find any old photos of Sarah Ellender. Hilda said, "Why, we sure did. Have you never seen them? There is a family group picture of her with her parents and all her brothers and sisters. I keep it in a hat box on the top shelf in the closet. I have been meaning to get all those old pictures organized, with names attached to all of them. If they aren't identified, then after we're all gone, no one will even know who is who." Ann nodded in agreement.

The face in the blurry old picture showed an attractive lady with a high-collared dress, in late-1800s attire. She stood beside her brother, the one identified as John H. Winters. He was Sarah Ellender's favorite brother as the family story went, and there was no doubt the *H* stood for Henry because she named her youngest son with Samuel, John Henry. Her face was pretty, and she appeared to be in her thirties or so.

Jane swallowed hard and tried to remain composed. *It's her. Just as sure as I am standing here, it's her,* Jane thought with wide eyes. *It's the lady in the mirror.* A chill ran down her spine, and the color drained a bit from her cheeks. Jane took a long breath.

What was Sarah Ellender trying to tell her? What was she trying so hard to convey? Never had anything such as this happened to Jane, and she did not quite know what to make of it.

This is something that I just don't need to tell anyone, not yet anyway, she thought with surety. *Not until I can wrap my brain around it. Folks will start thinking you are completely loony when you start blabbing about stuff like this.* So, taking a deep breath, she kept her revelation to herself.

After a rousing afternoon and evening of festive laughing, talking, and, of course, sampling the delicious goodies, Jane slept in the living room on the folding couch and slept soundly. It was the first truly deep sleep she had gotten in months. She woke in the morning light to Ann's smiling face looking down at her with a steaming cup of coffee in her hand.

"Morning, sugar!" Ann happily called out. "Tell me you are going to stay with us awhile today, and not rush right back up the mountain?"

Jane sure wanted to get back, and soon. She realized that she missed the place. "I'll stay awhile. I sure don't want to miss seeing Uncle Bill and Aunt Patsy," Jane replied. "Are they still coming over at lunchtime?"

"They sure are," Hilda sang out in her musical Carolina twang. "They will be upset if you miss seeing them, you know they will now," she said beseechingly.

Uncle Bill enjoyed being right in the middle of his doting sisters. He had kept this a guarded secret for years, of course, with feigned indifference to all the attention. And, as always, he was taken extra-special care of, being the younger brother. A kindly soul, he and sweet Aunt Patsy, were also very special to Jane.

Patsy, being the younger sister, also was given extra love and attention by Ann, and Hilda, too. Jane smiled as she watched the siblings' loving interactions. Jane thought that her sweet aunt Patsy looked more and more like her grandmother Maude, every day.

Patsy was always quilting, sewing, or making something beautiful. She was very talented at such things. Seeing the resemblance so evident in Patsy's looks and mannerisms comforted Jane immensely. No doubt it comforted the others as well. It was times like this that she missed her dad the most. He would have loved seeing them all together again, and he would have loved being right in the center of it all. He truly loved his family and especially the laughter that rang out in the house when they were all together.

Jane waited until after everyone had eaten, and Bill and Patsy had left before she started packing up her suitcase and gathering her belongings.

Ann saw that she was beginning to pack, and she sat down on the bed, she said, "I worry about you, all by yourself in that drafty old house. All alone up there on that snowy ol' mountain. You've been alone up there, for weeks at a time. Tell me that you will try and phone me, at least every other day. If you can't, I'll understand, but what if something happens to you, and we don't know that you need help?"

Hilda nodded in agreement. "We can't help but worry about our Janie," she said, smiling.

Jane thought to herself, *Well, whatever happens, Sarah Ellender will take care of me. There doesn't seem to be much that she can't handle.* But she refrained from saying any of that aloud. *That would raise two sets of eyebrows in a hurry, for sure, girlfriend*, Jane told herself. *These two can raise enough of a fuss without any extra help from me.*

So instead Jane said, "Now, you two, I appreciate you worrying so about me, but I will be just fine." And from the pouts that both had on their faces, Jane could easily tell that she had not given them the answer they had wanted.

Whatever reason Sarah Ellen had in trying to communicate this way remained to be seen, but Jane would sure appreciate any help she could get.

In the back of her mind, she secretly hoped that her dad would be the next to contact her. If there was a way, she knew her daddy would find it. He would try to help her understand it all, whatever message they were trying to convey, she just knew it. She felt compelled to return as quickly as possible, back to the house, with this thought.

You are losing it, girl. Get a grip. She laughed lightly out loud, and both Ann and Hilda shot her a questioning glance, and then quickly looked at each other with matching raised eyebrows.

Oops. Nothing much gets by these two, Jane thought.

Jane said her good-byes, hugged and kissed everyone, and after a few trips loaded the car and left. She headed back up the highway toward the misty mountain. The mountain that she now knew, without the slightest doubt, was her home.

6

The golden moments in the stream of life rush past us and we see nothing but sand; the angels come to visit us, and we only know them when they are gone.

~GEORGE ELLIOT

Back at the house, after traveling slow with snow chains wrapped around her tires, she sighed with relief as she finally was able to light the wood she had carefully stacked in the fireplace. *Home at last!* Jane thought happily. *All this, and a roaring fire, too.* While she was gone, the local fellow that had been recommended to her had come up and done a visual inspection of the old chimney and told her it was fine to use the fireplace.

"No bats, everything OK," read the note stuck to the pane of glass in the front door.

"Thank goodness," she had breathed aloud. The crackling fire in the fireplace quickly dispelled the chill in the room and added a cozy feel.

"Home. Daddy, can you believe it? This house is now, really and truly, my home," Jane announced happily to the room.

She quickly brought in the rest of her things from the car along with the tin of fruitcake that Hilda had packed up for her. Then she remembered the old gun still wrapped in the cloth and slid underneath the passenger seat. She ran back out and grabbed it, and ran back inside, stomping the snow off her feet onto the mat by the door, and quickly rushed over to warm herself by the massive old fireplace. The stones of the fireplace were beautiful. Each one placed carefully, with precision. It was built to last forever. *And I hope it does*, she thought. *I know that even long after I am gone, these rocks will still stand*. It soothed her heart to think that. As she stood admiring the stonework, she noticed one stone that appeared to have loose mortar surrounding it. She made a mental note to repair it soon.

Later, she took the gun and placed it in an old round-top steamer trunk that she had found last week in the walk-in closet off the main floor bedroom. The old trunk's worn leather straps were still intact but in need of replacing. She added to her mental note to purchase some leather as well.

The chest was empty when she found it, and still in pretty good shape, and she planned on using it.

She was truly tired from her full day, and when the shadows fell long across the mountain, and twilight settled in, she changed into a nightshirt and went on to bed. Jane lay down on the antique iron bedstead, snuggled down deep under the heavy old quilt, and fell asleep quickly. The wind shifted, and the music carried itself again over the mountain, floating on the cold winter wind, without any living soul ever hearing it.

The pine trees swayed and murmured in the starlit night, with only the clouds there to witness it. The music played until the wee hours of the morning. The high-timbered strains of a fiddle filled the cold night air and then a lonesome voice joined in. "Just a few more weary days and then I'll fly away, I'll fly away. When I die, hallelujah, by and by, I'll fly away." The sound of the lively banjo carried down the mountain in unison with the fiddle, and then down even further into the valley below. Jane slept soundly on, never hearing a note.

In the following days, she resumed her work and used the snowy days to accomplish as much as possible. *Staying focused and indoors is pretty easy, since it's so darn cold outside,* Jane thought with a shiver. She used an old oil lamp for light when the snow swirled thick, and the daylight was mostly blocked out. It seemed that the whole world was closed off from her, as the storm raged outside. What must it have been like, with a huge brood of children stuck inside with no chance of venturing outside to play? With no TV or Internet to help out, that must have tried the patience of any sainted mother. "Whew," Jane said aloud, shaking her head at the thought.

She ventured up the stairs one day, after scrubbing down more of the wood downstairs and then making a few small repairs in the drywall. She ascended the first few steps carefully, watching and feeling for weak spots in the risers. The newel post felt smooth and worn under her fingertips. Countless hands had worn the wood satiny smooth to the touch. She saw the indentions that footsteps had made into the wood of the risers.

Amazing, Jane thought. *Countless years of footsteps climbing these stairs have left these marks.* Feeling the boards sway and give beneath her, she quickly decided not to venture up any further.

She had spent most of her time in the house, and the past few weeks had been uneventful. Jane began to wonder if her overactive imagination had, in fact, simply conjured up the image in the mirror and the record-playing incident with Patsy's crooning. "Well, it's about time to forget all that nonsense. Ain't nobody here now but us chickens," she kidded herself.

Still standing at the base of the steps, she quickly had a strong sensation that someone was watching her, someone just over her shoulder. The hairs on her neck stood up on end and waved a cheery "hello!" to one another. Jane gulped in air, gathered her resolve, and slowly turned around. She saw nothing. Nothing looked amiss.

Dim light streamed in through the windows up above her and illuminated the stairs. She could see the dust in the air, swirling in the shaft of sunlight streaming down. Just as quickly as it came, the sensation left her. "You are seriously losing it, you ninny," she said breathlessly and laughed to herself. She took a deep breath and stood there for a moment, trying to reassure herself, slowly dismissing the feeling.

Further down the hall, in the shadows, the edge of a long dark dress hem swung around, sweeping soundlessly across the floor as if someone wearing it had turned suddenly and walked away. Jane never saw it, but the dust swirled in the hall for just a moment longer, and then settled back down.

After taking another close look at the stairs, she decided not to go up any further. Some of the boards were in pretty bad shape, and she did not want to risk falling through and breaking an ankle. There was no one here to help her if she did. So she turned and carefully came back down the few risers, her hand resting lightly on the smooth old newel post. She stood and thought, *Old houses are like time capsules with each generation leaving its own imprint, year after year.* She just loved old things because of that. This love was deep within her, inspired by her father. "Old things could tell you quite a story, if they would," he would often say.

Even an old sugar bowl has stories. It sits on the table and sees everything that happens around that table, and that home, year after year, and generation after generation. "Even that small chipped sugar bowl could tell you a lot," he would reason. His voice still echoed in her memory from time to time.

I suppose he was right about that, Jane thought to herself. *Dad was right about a lot of things.*

Jane's mind wandered back to her Grandma Maudie's sugar bowl. She would let Jane help her in the kitchen when she was very young. *I am not so sure I was ever actually that much help,* Jane thought, smiling. *More of a little 'Miss Mess Maker', I would say.*

She remembered standing up in the chair, just tall enough to reach the tabletop. Grandma would let her stir the batter. She would dip a battered fingertip into the sugar bowl and lick it off. Grandma kept a sugar bowl especially for little girls with sticky fingers. Grandmas really do let you get away with a lot; she had realized as she grew older, but as a child, she had thought it was perfectly normal to be spoiled nearly rotten.

Grandma's sugar bowl was filled with love, and her special kind of "sugar" spilled out on everyone around her. *There must be an extra special place in heaven for grandmas like mine.* Jane was lost deep in her thoughts. *I miss her, and Dad, so much*, she thought. *I imagine them having a long chat over a cup of coffee, sitting at the table with Grandma's sugar bowl between them.*

Sharing time and talk and, most of all, love, over that precious sugar bowl. How she wished, that one day, she could be a part of that sharing, with them both, up in heaven.

The next morning, Jane was busy scrubbing the wavy old glass panes in the front windows. The windows extended from the floor to the ceiling, and the glass appeared to be original to construction. Suddenly, on the other side of the window, a red cardinal flew up and landed on the sill. Then it cocked its head to the side and peered in at Jane. Jane's hand paused in mid-swipe, and she put her handful of vinegar-dipped newspaper down on the table. She had been using it all morning since she had run out of the regular cleaner, realizing that it did work just as well, maybe even better.

She smiled at the cardinal and said, "Now, Mr. Red Bird, you sure are handsome with those bright red feathers." The cardinal suddenly turned and, with wings outspread, flew at the glass and crashed into it, beak first. It floundered about and then flung itself hard once again, at the glass, seemingly frantic to get inside.

Alarmed, Jane cried out and backed up quickly, nearly falling over a bucket of water that sat just behind her. When she had time to catch her breath, she thought with a grin, *That scared the mush right out of me, and then I think I hit a high* C. Those were Aunt Ann's words, no doubt, and she had sounded just like her.

Jane giggled nervously. *What in the world would have caused the bird to behave like that?* There was no actual direct light that would have allowed the bird to see its own reflection, but that is what Jane decided must have happened. It had scared itself and flung its body at the pane, to protect itself from the bird it saw in the window. But in the back of her mind, Jane remembered that a bird trying to gain entry into a house through a window was a bad sign. It was a very bad sign, indeed.

I'm not going to let myself worry about any old wives' tales, Jane thought. *Not today, not here, alone in an old house, full of creaking boards and unsettled ghosts. That bird just saw itself in the glass. End of subject.* She laughed nervously to herself. *Now, girlie, let's just file that away and forget it, shall we?*

As she finished the windows and moved onto the washing of the windowsills, Jane felt some better. *You just cannot let this spooky business get the better of you.* She could almost envision her dad's smiling face. He would have laughed heartily at her, for sure. *Enough of this silliness*, she thought to herself.

Just as she turned to get a clean rag to dip into the wood polish, she heard the music. It suddenly filled the entire room. It was way too loud to have come from anywhere but right inside the house. A hauntingly solemn voice rang out with the sound of a mandolin playing melody.

"I'm just a poor wayfaring stranger. I'm traveling through this world of woe. Yet there's no sickness, toil nor danger, in that bright land to which I go. I'm going there to see my father, I'm going there no more to roam."

And just as quickly as the sound came, it died quietly away. Jane felt as if she could not breathe. She was stuck where she was standing, with feet frozen, afraid to move. *OK, there is no way I just imagined that.* It was as if she could feel the vibration of the voice, still in the air. Suspended like a feather that wouldn't drop. A feather, gently lifted up and lightly floating downward, but still there, never quite falling back to the ground.

She knew that tune. It was an old bluegrass tune that her father had sometimes sung while he was tinkering with something. It was a tune that was comforting to him, and dear. It was comforting to her, as well. She had loved to hear her father sing that while he worked; sometimes he whistled it. Could that have been his voice? She was so startled that she felt addled. *I just need to get out of this house for a while*, she thought with as much calm as she could muster. She wasted no time bundling up warmly, with several layers of clothing and then added an extra knitted scarf. Out the door and down the path she walked, through the crunchy snow.

Out in the brisk, clean air she instantly felt better. She ventured up the trail further than she had gone before, and she saw up ahead that the trees gave way to a clearing. Once she was upon a small ridge, she paused to catch her breath. Jane did not even realize that a silly smile was plastered on her face. The trail wound its way up the ridge and probably connected with the Appalachian Trail, before going much further. The trees here were magnificent, ancient and towering overhead, and her steps made hollow-sounding echoes because of the dense layers of pine needles underfoot, deep beneath the snow.

It was so peaceful out here on this mountainside, and she just loved being here, soaking in that wonderful peace. The fresh air scented with rich, sweet pine greeted her the moment she walked outside. She could think straighter out here than she ever could inside of any house. The unrest that came from being cooped up indoors had come from her Indian blood on the Correll side. At least she had always thought so. That is what her dad had always told her, ever since she was just a little girl. She sometimes just knew, inexplicably, that certain things were going to happen. She simply "knew" a lot of things, and she was sure that it ran in her family line.

Her grandmother had once told her about a dream she had, and she had described the very same dream that Jane herself had dreamed, just days earlier. It was quite unnerving at the time, but over the years she had begun to accept her strange dreams and forewarnings. She had always thought of it as her guardian angels, whispering into her ear, and gently guiding her path.

Just as she thought about the dreams, she felt the sensation of eyes upon her. She slowed her steps along the path and turned around. Looking behind, she saw nothing, but eyes remained upon her nonetheless. She hurried up a bit further along the path and into the clearing. She thought for sure someone or something was following her. She felt the hair on the back of her neck prickle.

She walked past a large weathered pine tree, and she caught sight of an unusual shape, close to the ground in the underbrush. She ventured further, pushing old dried vines out of the way. There, just out of the tree line, was a grave marker. There were several more just beyond it. She could see them more clearly as she bent down lower, peeking through the thick growth of old honeysuckle vines and dead sumac. The name on one of the stones was clearly legible. *Correll*.

It was an old family burying ground. One that she had never heard spoken of, by the family. She had not realized it was right here on the property, and so close to the house. She had begun wondering about the family she came from when she was just a teenager, and her dad had told her enough to satisfy her curiosity at the time. But she was sure that she did not remember ever being told about a family graveyard, right here, within sight of the house.

Wonder why Dad didn't ever mention this to me? Had he not known it was here? Were these souls buried after Dad had married and moved away? Surely these markers are older than that. Jane's mind rifled through several possible explanations, but she could not decide which seemed plausible.

No first name was discernible on the marker closest to her, and the rest were fully covered by a tangle of vines. It would require some clippers or even a hatchet to clear away this mess, neither of which she had brought with her on this walk. So, this would have to wait for another day. Besides, her hands were like blocks of ice from the fierce, icy wind that was howling up the mountainside. With the wind whistling past her ears, she could almost believe she heard the strains of fiddle music wafting toward her again.

Shaking her head to get rid of the sound that she thought she must be imagining, she turned back toward the house and to some much-needed warmth. Her legs began to tickle and feel odd. Her family also had another strange trait. *Allergic to the cold, of all strange things*, Jane thought. Not only did her fingertips turn blue at the slightest drop in temperature, but her legs would swell in large patches and itch like mad if she got too cold. "Strange family, indeed," she chuckled. "Allergic to cold, now who would believe that, besides an Arrowood?"

Back at the house, she warmed herself by the fireplace and stoked the embers to a red-hot glow. *Much better now*, she thought. With her hands extended out to the fire, the color soon returned to her fingers, and the itching subsided. She allowed herself to wonder again about the graves out in the brambles. *Who are they and why were they buried right here, and not over on Shell Creek with the rest of the family?* She toyed with several scenarios for quite a while but ended up at a loss for an explanation.

She cleaned, scrubbed, spackled, polished, and repaired until the winter's fierce hold on the mountain slowly began to loosen. The frozen scene outside her door reluctantly gave way to an almost warm sunshine and the earth finally sprouted green shoots from underneath the thick melting snow. Every morning when she awoke she thought for sure that the smell of spring was clearer to her. The house was coming along nicely, and she couldn't believe the transformation. It was as if it had a life of its own now, and the restoration was being very much welcomed. Jane was very pleased, very pleased indeed.

She had almost allowed herself to forget the strange happenings and decided to try to push them out of her mind, entirely. She had wondered, more than once, if she was slowly losing her marbles or something even worse.

The lady that ran a quaint little antique shop in town had told her about a local man who would replace the porch for her at a reasonable rate. She went to the town hall to find this local man's sister, as she had been instructed. She talked with Gwen, the lady behind the counter, who promised to send her brother Jake over to the house first thing in the morning. Satisfied that the new porch would soon be completed, Jane felt bolstered that another major repair was that much closer to being complete.

Next morning, as promised, Jake arrived. He knocked on the front door as Jane was in the kitchen making coffee. She opened the door and saw a man a little older than herself with undeniable good looks. *Now, come on. Why does he have to be this good-looking? I would have been fine with a typical local yokel. But no, I have to go and get this ridiculously handsome man. Why me?* Jane groaned inwardly.

Jane had been dealt a lousy hand with men more than once, and she had no intention of being dealt another. *No entanglements for me, not ever again*, she had thought to herself, time after time. She tried to remain cool and collected, but it was sure hard. Jake was very well mannered and just as good-looking as he was polite. Jane secretly hoped that he'd ask her to tomorrow's town dance that she had heard about a few days prior, it sure sounded like fun. It had taken her only about ten seconds to notice there was no ring on his finger.

She instantly wished that she had paid a little more attention to her appearance. This morning she had just twisted up her hair and not much else. *With the men that I have seen around town, who knew there was a drop-dead-gorgeous fix-it man cruising around these parts unprotected?* she thought with a nervous giggle.

Jake asked her to go to the dance with him within ten minutes of first meeting her. She had no way of knowing it, but Jake was more than a little smitten with her, at very first glance.

7

Give sorrow words; the grief that does not speak whispers the o'er-fraught heart and bids it break.

~WILLIAM SHAKESPEARE

The Cabin

THE WIND HOWLED outside the little cabin, and a freezing-cold blast of air blew under the door with a vengeance. Nancy shuddered and drew her worn shawl closer around her shoulders. She walked to the window and peered out, searching the woods for any glimpse of David making his way home. Even though the path leading up to the cabin was obscured by snow, she knew the way well. David was out there, somewhere, searching for game to bring home to the hungry family.

Nancy's eyes softened as she watched the little one playing on the blanket beside the fire. The wood pile was getting lower and lower with each passing day, and she had begun to ration herself, trying to stretch it out as best she could. She ran her hand over her belly and smiled. The coming baby prevented her from chopping much wood. She'd had enough trouble with the first one, and she wanted to take no chances this time. She brushed her long, dark hair away from her face and sighed.

She wished that David did not have to stay out there alone, in the cold for days on end. The soldiers came over the mountain and watched the cabin just about every day now. They knew David would return eventually, and they wanted to force him into fighting in this terrible war. She knew that David "had no dog in this fight," just as she had heard him say a hundred times, at least. The simple mountain folk that lived in the area owned no slaves, and most felt that the war was simply none of their affair. This war was a rich man's war, and certainly they were not rich.

Going off to war would not put food on the table. How could he leave his family hungry? David knew they would starve to death with him gone, or even freeze to death, and easily. David would never let either happen, but what if something bad did happen to him? Nancy was terrified to let herself think something like that, but she knew down deep that it was very possible, as well.

Nancy and David were totally devoted to each other, and the idea of living without the other was just unthinkable. Their love ran deep and true, and they had felt this way since they were both just children.

Nancy went out into the cold air, with her breath rising in puffs of steam around her head. She carefully made her way down the frozen steps and out to the clothesline. The mattress made of straw, and covered with worn cotton cloth, was the signal that they used. David knew it was safe to come back to the cabin if the mattress was hanging. Without the sign in place, he would stay in hiding. He knew then that the soldiers were still nearby.

Nancy scanned the hillside as she hurried to hang the mattress. Her fingers were so cold, and she only had the pockets of her apron to ball her fists into, to try and warm them as she made her way back inside.

This war has to end sometime, she thought to herself. *It just can't go on forever.* She was scared of the soldiers lurking about, and each time they came, she tried not to look directly at any of them.

Any woman living alone on this mountain has plenty to worry about these days. There is no safety when your man is off in the woods somewhere, she thought. It was just not right that he could not be here with them, especially since the baby was getting close to coming, and there was no one else within walking distance. Most had left months ago.

Nancy was a beautiful woman, but the constant worry was beginning to show on her young face. Life here was hard, and it had begun to take its toll on the girl. Her sunken cheeks were pale, and her dress was beginning to hang on her thin frame, despite the baby bulge.

She knew the potatoes that she had grown this past summer were running low, but there were still some sound cabbages left and some wild locusts. There were just a few dozen apples left, as well. She had her small crop of root vegetables buried in the ground, in a row down near the creek. She had taken the cabbage and vegetables and buried them upside down in the soft dirt, and then she had nestled straw in around them. It was called "holing up" the vegetables, by most folks. It was an effective method of preservation during harsh winters, providing almost fresh cabbage and produce in the dead of winter.

Nancy constantly scanned the area around her for soldiers. They would frequently come by, looking for deserters and those mountain men who figured they need not participate in a fight they did not consider their own. Most had labeled them all as dirty deserters and cowards. That made Nancy fighting mad whenever she thought about it. Her David was no deserter, nor was he a coward. How could they call him a deserter when he never agreed with it from the beginning and never joined up? The soldiers would do just about whatever they wanted to when they came. They would even take their food and leave them hungry, and Nancy offered up little resistance. It angered her plenty, them taking food from the mouth of her little one and herself, but she knew that there was little she could do to stop it. *At least the vegetables that are buried are safe and out of sight*, she thought with a sigh.

David had gone hunting for meat at least four days ago. *Oh, where is he? Please, dear Lord, keep him safe.* Her lips moved in silent prayer.

The mountain area's dissatisfaction with the war had begun early in this year of 1862. The mountain people all felt that the Confederate government had discriminated against the poorer people, unjustly. These people were just dirt farmers—they owned precious little and certainly not any slaves, so they had no valid reason to fight in this war. The heavy-handed enforcement of the military enraged these poor farmers, and many hid out up in the hills to keep from being forced to fight.

Guerilla bands roamed the mountains and molested and pillaged as they went. Most in the area called them bushwhackers. The little food that was available was taken, and no thought was given to the family left hungry, and without. The mountain people suffered, and no one outside the area even seemed to notice. Nancy knew that she must be ever on guard. So she and David devised a system of signals to communicate with each other. The water bucket turned upside down and left on the porch, by the door, meant trouble. A rag tied on the door or onto a tree branch in the yard meant something had happened, and Nancy had to leave the cabin.

David was just twenty-two years old in 1862 and young Nancy only twenty.

With the new baby coming later in the summer, Nancy worried about having yet another mouth to feed. She knew what plants were edible, and she made stews and soups with whatever she had to stretch out the potatoes and vegetables she had managed to save in the soil. *What doesn't rot, it seems that the rats always have a go at*, she thought with a sigh. She dug up a few vegetables, picking through what was left and washed the soil off in the creek water.

She used melted snow when the creek froze over, so at least she did not have to worry about water. She turned to hurry back inside the cabin and suddenly and soundlessly there appeared a soldier just ahead, on the creek bank. Standing perfectly still, he was between her and the cabin, blocking the path and peering down on her without ever speaking a word.

She sharply sucked in a breath and tightened her grip on the vegetable sack.

"Well, what do we have here, fellers?" She noticed movement out of the corner of her eye, and she saw three more soldiers were moving closer to her. Four men total. She knew this was bad.

She called out to the cabin, "David, we have company!" Holding her chin up proudly, Nancy acted a world braver than she felt. David was nowhere near, and she knew there was no one to help her now. She was on her own, and she had to keep her wits about her somehow.

She drew in a ragged breath, squared her shoulders, and pretended to be calm. She scrambled up the bank, slipping in the mud and then walked stiffly by the soldier, passing him on the path. Feeling anything but calm, Nancy said, "My husband will be out to talk to you shortly, sir."

"Husband?" snorted the soldier. "Why, a young thing like you surely ain't got herself no husband. You're way too purty to be out here all alone, now ain't you?"

He reached out and grabbed her wrist and wrenched her closer to him. Nancy stumbled as she lost her balance. The others circled in closer and slowly they all began to laugh low and exchange glances.

8

Come, ye disconsolate, where'er you languish,
Come at the shrine of God fervently kneel;
Here bring your wounded hearts, here tell your anguish—
Earth has no sorrow that Heaven cannot heal.

~Thomas Moore

The sun was sinking low in the sky when Nancy finally awoke, hours later. She lay on the frozen ground with her dress muddied and ripped off her shoulder. Her clothing was hanging in tatters around her waist. Her tears had dried on her swollen face and, thankfully, the soldiers had left. She struggled to her feet, wincing in pain. She managed to stand, holding her bruised and battered belly in her hands. They had not only violated her but in the fight that ensued, beaten her unconscious. She suddenly gasped as she remembered little Isabelle, left alone in the cabin. She slid in the muck and almost fell, unsteady on her feet, trying to run up the path to the house. She stumbled up onto the porch and slammed back the door and saw Isabelle still playing happily on the hearth by the fire.

She was safe and completely unaware of what had happened. Nancy silently thanked God for that. She stumbled over to the chair and sat down, holding her bleeding, throbbing head. Blood had dried on her lip where the soldier had ruthlessly bitten her. She bowed her head in prayer once again, "Thank you, God, for allowing my baby girl to remain unharmed." She began to cry softly, and her shoulders heaved in torment. "They had no right to take my body. They had no right at all."

God only knows what those monstrous men would have done if they had known the child was here. With that thought, Nancy shuddered. *Thank God, she didn't cry or make a sound.* She watched little Isabelle quietly play with her corn-husk dolly, her angelic face lit with the glow from the fire.

David was cold, tired, and his brow was deeply furrowed in worry. He never stopped thinking about his Nancy. *This war is causing us all to starve*, he thought. His main thought was getting some meat on the table, and soon. The talk among the others, who were in the same predicament was that things were probably going to be worse before they got any better.

He heard one fellow tell that there was a farmer over in the next county that somehow had gotten himself two uniforms, a Rebel one, and a Confederate one. That way, when he saw the marauders a-comin' toward the cabin, he would put on the right uniform coat and sit out on the porch and wait for 'em. "Whatever tactic that saves what little you have left, works for me," David reasoned.

Not only do we have to contend with the thieving soldiers, but we have to be on the lookout for desperate deserters as well. Everyone's starving, including me, young David thought, thin as a rail. *This whole world has likely as not gone stark-raving mad, fighting a'gin one another whether they be neighbors or even brothers, raised up in the same family home. What place does someone like me have in this madness? This surely ain't my war, and I don't want to have to fight for something that ain't no affair of my own.*

The deserter camp was not very far from David and Nancy's little cabin. Being in such close proximity to a band of desperate men worried David fiercely, but there was little he could do about it, but try to keep a close watch on them. What with another mouth to feed coming soon, David worried even more.

Staying away from his home was the hardest thing he had ever done in his short life. But being forced into fighting this war would mean certain starvation for his beloved Nancy, and he was determined not to let that happen.

David had never run away from a fight in his life; it went against his very nature. But leaving his family to fend for themselves with men running around looting for food and goodness knows what all else? Well, it was just not going to happen. *If'n the government sees fit to label me a coward for taking care of my own, well, so be it!* he thought.

At night, the torch lights from the deserter camp could be seen glowing from across the rise of the hill. It was the last thing David saw as he lay down to sleep. But most nights, sleep eluded David, and when he did sleep, the war loomed ever closer in his fitful dreams. He had found a small cave nearby that he had fashioned into a makeshift shelter. The wind howled down the mountain, but the cave at least afforded him a wind break. The lighting of a fire for warmth or cooking was a large risk, one that he did not often take. Being alone meant no one was there to help if he was attacked. He may have to resort eventually to joining up with the camp, but for now, he chose to stay to himself. It seemed safer here. News of the war edging ever closer filtered down through occasional encounters with passersby on the trail and David thought it best to lie as low as possible for the time being.

Another passerby was heading his way this very moment. As he came closer to the man, he could see that he was dust covered and grimy from countless days on the trail.

The man called out to David. "Howdy. Now, I ain't got me no gun, mind you. I'm just wantin' to pass on by you, right peaceful like. Don't mean no harm to you. No harm a'tall."

David acknowledged him with a smile and a nod, tipping his tattered hat, and then stuck out his hand to shake. "No fight I'll give you, friend." The man let out a sigh of relief, they shook hands, and he sat down on a large rock by the trail. He took off his hat and wiped his brow with his handkerchief. "I have heard tell that them bushwhackers are attacking innocent women and children, now. There's just no end to the misery, son." The man shook his head disconsolately and then quickly looked back up the path, in the direction he had just come.

The sound of horses, coming fast, reached David's ears then, too. They both scurried off the path and into the woods to hide. The horses thundered past with both men unseen, standing behind large trees about thirty feet into the forest.

Five riders with household goods tied to their saddles passed by, riding fast. The man slowly ventured out of his hiding place and came nearer to David through the trees.

He said, "Them was bushwhackers, no doubt in my mind about it. I recognized the belongings of a woman what fed me, just a while back, tied up to their saddles. No telling what they did to her. That poor kindly soul that offered me food, just because I was hungry, now is more 'n likely dead. She barely had enough to keep herself fed. These are powerful evil days."

The man tipped his hat to David and said, "God go with you, son", and as quickly as he had appeared on the path, he was gone.

David saw not another living soul for three days after meeting the stranger. It seemed to David that even the rabbits were in hiding as he checked trap, after empty trap. Every snapping twig echoed loudly through the trees, and David had never felt so alone.

In his mind's eye, he saw Nancy warm by the fire, safely holding a sleeping Isabelle. *That is what I will focus on*, he thought, *instead of my growling belly and my cold feet.*

9

Lord, 'tis Thy plenty-dropping hand
That soils my land,
And giv'st me for my bushel sowne
Twice ten for one.
All this, and better, Thou dost send
Me, to this end,
That I should render, for my part,
A thankful heart.

~Robert Herrick

BACK IN PRESENT day, up on the Roan, Jane busied herself with a platter of veggies. *Something quick and easy*, she thought. Dressed in a little ice blue sleeveless dress, she was almost ready for the dance. She wanted to try and fit in, because after all, this was going to be her home. She had decided on a whim, to wear her special shoes. She was feeling a bit brave and daring. Her shoes were just exactly what her grandmother Maude would have chosen, had she been there to help her with her outfit. They were clear, lucite heels that were embedded with rhinestones. They were without a doubt, totally over the top and certainly, " Maudacious". Jane chuckled to herself as she slipped the shoes on and admired them. She thought for sure that people would stare at them, maybe even think she was nuts, but she didn't really mind. It was almost a comfort thinking that her "Maudie" shoes were finally going to be worn. Grandma would have just loved it.

Most of the ladies there will bring in their famous treasured recipes, and here I am with cut-up carrots and dip. "Geez, how original," she said and laughed. "Oh, well. They will just have to understand that my kitchen is not all that operational yet." She grimaced slightly. The kitchen table was still strewn with hammers and wood polish these days. *Surely, just the fact that I even came should be a feather in my cap in the eyes of the locals*, Jane thought. Mountain folk tend to be wary of outsiders, even if they are the kids of families that have been here for generations. Every newcomer would come under scrutiny, and she knew it.

A knock on the door signaled the butterflies to commence their flight of fancy deep in her midsection. Nervous jitters, first date, and a platter of plain old veggies, it all was just about too much for her. Jane took a deep breath, plastered a smile on her face and opened the door. Jake stood there with his cowboy hat in his hand. *This amount of handsome just has to be illegal in most states*, Jane thought with a wry smile spreading across her lips. *Boy howdy, and then some.*

Still smiling, she lowered her head so he could not possibly read her thoughts, grabbed her purse, and climbed into his truck. She moved carefully up into the seat, mindful of her short dress. Then down the mountain to town they went.

The music was loud inside the tiny town hall. *The atmosphere in here is positively electric*, Jane thought, as she walked inside. *Well, as "electric" as it can get in this tiny little village*, she reconsidered with a smile. It was crowded inside, so Jane figured just about everyone in town had made it out to the "big to-do." There was no doubt that being snowed in for the long winter caused the townsfolk to eagerly attend any function at all. *Sure can't blame them*, she thought.

Jake introduced her around and for the most part, the folks were surprisingly friendly. Most of the older women cast lingering sidelong glances at Jane, but that is what women always do to younger girls. She smiled at everyone, and she soon determined to make the most of the evening. The food was without a doubt, awesome. *The people here can sure cook. I guess I had better step up my game for the next bash.*

The music was lively and after being swirled around the dance floor in a jaunty two-step, Jane found herself laughing and out of breath.

Mrs. Miller, who lived just across the hollow, walked over and introduced herself. She asked her about the progress she was making on the house repairs. Jane smiled and chatted easily with her. After making pleasant conversation, Mrs. Miller abruptly changed her demeanor and pulled Jane aside, and said rather bluntly, "You just need to watch yourself, miss. Strange happenings in that house over the years have given it a quite a reputation. We are all just about convinced that it is haunted or something even worse," she said matter-of-factly.

Jane raised her eyebrows slightly with a smile and then tried to dismiss the notion. But she thanked her kindly for the information, just the same. *Well, seems the whole town thinks my house is infested with ghosts. But considering the upside, maybe that will keep them from bothering me so much*, Jane thought, smiling to herself.

Jake was quite a character and proved to be quite entertaining, all evening long, and they both enjoyed the night immensely. She didn't want to see it come to an end. They danced to nearly every song, and even the "John Paul Jones" was lively. Jane hadn't had that much fun in a long time.

Jake drove her back home in the darkness, and when he took her to the front door, he bent down and kissed her lightly on the lips. She did not resist. The light of the moon illuminated the porch brightly. They both turned and looked up at it. "What do you think is really up there?" Jake asked.

Jane said, "There's no telling. There just has to be so much more that has yet to be discovered. Sometimes I think that some things prefer just to stay hidden away."

Jake looked at her quizzically and smiled. "You are one different kind of lady, up here in this creaky old house all alone. But I do like determination in a woman. I like it just fine." Jane smiled and this time she kissed him lightly.

"I enjoyed the dance," he said. "I would love to see you again, and soon."

Jane said, "Well, we will just have to see how things go from here." They both smiled, and then Jake walked over to his truck and got in. Jane stood on the porch and watched. He got back out of the truck and walked over to kiss her lightly on the cheek.

"What was that for?" she asked.

"That was for saving me from Mrs. Miller. She was going to ask me about her confounded sticking door for about the fiftieth time. I fixed that dang ol' door two months ago, but she has forgotten that I was even there. Old-timers, I guess." Jake grinned. Jane laughed lightly and stood at the door and watched as he drove away.

This was a good night, maybe even a new beginning, she thought.

She turned and went inside the house and lit a fire in the fireplace, replaying the night's events in her mind as she watched the embers glow until she fell fast asleep.

The sunlight streaming across her face woke her.

I never even made it to bed last night, she thought with a yawn. She was still lying on the couch. Her neck was stiff from the awkward angle in which she had fallen asleep. She walked into the kitchen, rubbing her neck, and in the bright morning light, she saw through fresh eyes what a mess it had somehow become. She started to clear away the clutter and sweep up the sawdust, and then she thought better of it, and she put the broom down. She poured herself a cup of strong hot coffee. *First things first*, she thought. After the coffee, she tidied up and swept the floor.

Later that afternoon, she went into town and bought more supplies. Jake's crew was scheduled to start replacing the porch the following morning, and she knew she still needed a few more things.

While she was putting everything into the trunk of the car, a frail voice sounded from behind her. "Hello, again," Mrs. Miller said.

Oh, no, here it comes, Jane thought. She turned and smiled warmly at Mrs. Miller. Maybe she was still worried about her door, after all. Jane's smile slowly faded away when she saw her.

She had an odd, nearly blank expression on her face, and she spoke almost in a whisper. Her eyes were the eyes of a frightened child. "They want me to warn you, but I don't rightly know how. They want me to tell you that you need to listen to them, but I am not even sure who they are." Mrs. Miller seemed confused as to who *she* even was at that moment, and then she blurted out, "You just need to watch yourself!" She abruptly turned, walked over to her car and got in.

Jane just stood there clutching the bag of supplies. She watched Mrs. Miller back up her car and drive off, and she never looked back at her. "Mercy me," Jane whispered to herself. "That woman is out, just driving around, and she is no doubt someone that does not need to be driving. Maybe I need to mention this to the police. This is certainly not good."

She did wonder about what the lady had said. So many strange things had happened that dismissing yet another odd event was pretty hard. The cryptic message stuck in Jane's head for the rest of the day.

Jane drove down the road to the diner and turned into the tiny parking lot. Just a quick bite and she'd feel better, she felt sure. She parked in the first empty space and went inside. The atmosphere was instantly soothing. The smell of hot coffee and bread baking always made her feel better. She ordered the "blue plate special" as she walked past the waitress and slipped into a booth. The sunshine through the window had warmed up the red vinyl seat nicely. "Wonder if they charge extra for this?" she murmured under her breath. She smiled in contentment, arching her back like a cat against the soothing warmth of the seat.

Love and Mercy - Up On Roan Mountain

She had frozen almost all winter, and, quite honestly, that big old house was never truly as warm as she would have liked it to be. *I do need some good weatherproofing, some thick insulation, and, well, all that will come*, she thought to herself. The house needed new windows and a new roof, too, eventually. She saw it all in her mind's eye.

After eating and exchanging pleasantries with two of the ladies in town she had met at the dance, Jane paid her bill and went to the car. She drove back up the mountain and made several trips inside the house to bring in her new supplies. On the last trip out to the car, she heard the distinct sound of tires crunching on gravel. She turned and shielded her eyes from the sun to see who was pulling into the drive.

The truck was red and huge. It was Jake. She smiled. He got out and walked over and said, "You are the talk of the town, m'lady!"

"Why, whatever for?" Jane said in her best Scarlett O'Hara southern drawl, smiling broadly.

"The whole town is yammering on and on about you, ramblin' around in this big old house, with no one to watch out for you."

"Oh, I think I have it covered," Jane countered easily. "I'm a big girl, and this is my house now." She smiled up at him. And he smiled broadly at her and thought to himself, *I am going to marry this girl before someone else snaps her up for themselves.*

The thought was barely formed in his mind, and instantly Jake's eyes widened from the shock of it. He could not quite believe it was his own, as the smile slipped from his face. Jake felt that he was just not the type to commit to anything—not for very long, anyway. Definitely not marriage. He stopped short for a moment to gather his senses. *No sense tipping your hat this early in the game*, he warned himself. *This is no ordinary girl. She is in control, and she knows it. But time will tell*, he thought, and slowly smiled to himself. *Time will tell.*

Jane wondered why he was smiling like that. It was a smile that you'd expect to see on a cat that had a bird's feather sticking to the corner of its mouth. It made her more than a little self-conscious, but she tried hard not to let it show. She prided herself on being able to keep her playing cards close to her chest, and this time would prove to be no exception.

Her daddy had taught her a lot of things, but the main lesson she had learned was to stay in control of her own destiny. She was extremely determined to do just that.

My daddy sure didn't raise no fool, Jane thought with a grin. She did, on rare occasions, bat her long eyelashes, but only just a tad. *But no one ever said that you can't do that now and then.* It was Jane's turn to smile slyly, the same smile that Jake had used earlier.

He walked over, grabbed the bulk of the supplies left in the car, and helped her carry them into the house. He went about putting things up, and when he did not know where things were kept, he asked. Jane secretly appreciated his attempt to try and help. *It's a great start*, she thought.

They walked through the house room by room as she told him what she envisioned and what she hoped to accomplish. He smiled, nodded, and seemed actually to contemplate everything she said. *That is yet another fine trait. He's not forcing his opinion on me, this early on, and I appreciate it. Hmm, duly noted reserve. You just gotta love that in a man.*

At the base of the stairs, he looked up and saw that some of the risers were in need of replacement, and some were possibly quite dangerous. "How about this staircase?" Jake asked. "Have you made any attempts at repair on this?"

"No, not yet," Jane said. "I've focused on just the main floor first, and actually, I've only gone up partway, so far. They look to me as if they might give way at any given time."

"I think you're right," he said. "I can look at them and see what needs to be done if you want me to."

"I would appreciate it, but you must accept payment before I would even consider it," Jane said honestly.

"OK, Missy, I gladly accept your offer. Let's go see what it is that needs to happen up there and soon," Jake said. He then smiled and took her hand. Jane's face flushed instantly at his words. Seeing her reaction, he quickly rebounded and stammered, "I mean, let's see what needs to be fixed first." The color drained out of Jane's face when she suddenly realized that what he was implying was completely innocent.

When are you ever going to get a grip on how to deal with men? Like, never? she berated herself silently. Jake seemed to dismiss the awkward moment and went on talking about the course of repairs needed for the stairs.

As they both mounted the first riser, the wood creaked ominously beneath their combined weight. Jake stopped and said, "Hey, let me go first, and that way if anything decides suddenly to go south, you won't be hurt. If it holds me, surely you will be fine. Otherwise," Jake said, grinning, "please call 911 at your earliest convenience."

Jane waited down below as Jake tentatively took each step, one at a time. When he was safely at the top, he nodded for her to come up.

Once she was standing on the landing, she could see the bedrooms on either side. The larger one opened to the right, and from the view, she could see an old iron bed and another old trunk, pushed off into a corner. The trunk was an antique steamer type, with a rounded top.

She had read somewhere that the round-top trunks were typically of better quality than the regular flat-topped ones. The rounded-top trunks were always placed on top of the stacks, with the square flat-top ones below, when placed aboard ships. "Oh, Dad," she whispered to herself, thinking about how he would have loved to have heard the tale that this old trunk possessed.

She so badly wanted to fling it open to see what was inside. She nearly flew across the room, and much to her surprise, Jake must have felt the same way because he moved just as quickly toward it as she did.

Laughing, they both knelt down before the old trunk. Jane opened the latch, and after a quick glance at each other on an unspoken count of three, they both flung the top open.

Jane could not believe her eyes. Stacks and stacks of old letters, bound up with ribbons that had long since lost their color.

There were boxes stacked on one end of the trunk, and the sliding tray was full of small packages. Everything was carefully placed and appeared to have been treasured by someone. The smell of age and old paper was thick. This trunk had to have been here for quite some time and had not been opened in many years.

What was hidden here among the ribbon-wrapped envelopes? It was a veritable treasure trove, to Jane. *What stories are here, just waiting to be read?* Jane was beside herself with excitement. She peered down at the treasure before her. "Oh, Wow." She clasped her hands together. She turned to Jake, and he was carefully inspecting the lock. The treasures lay inside the trunk, not in the lock, Jane felt. He muttered something about "finding a locksmith in town who could probably make a new key if you wanted one."

He just didn't see it. Not the way Jane did, surely. Men. Women. How in the world were they supposed to get along, let alone live together? She rolled her eyes to the ceiling and said a quick count to ten to regain her composure.

Jake saw the mechanics of the trunk. He saw the lock, the missing key, the old box before them. Jane saw the mystery, the romance of the contents of the trunk. Men and women. *And never shall the two minds meet.* Jane sighed in resignation and thought it best just to let it go. *You can't have everything, girlie.* She smiled softly at the irony.

Just be happy for the gift of time with this wonderful, polite man and forget the fact that he is, after all, just a mere mortal. Jane blew her breath upward in an exasperated puff, and her hair fluffed out off her face. Looking at Jake she smiled. Jane then began fingering through the stacks. This would be a task of sheer joy. She wanted so badly to learn who her ancestors were, how they had lived their lives, and here, magically before her, was her very own honest-to-goodness "treasure chest" of info. Lovingly saved scraps and remnants of long-ago years, kept safe and tucked away, just waiting for her to come and find them. If her dad had known about this trunk, he had never, ever mentioned it to her.

If she had known this was here, nothing downstairs would have been done at all. She would have spent her days sitting in the rocking chair, right beside this trunk, reading and savoring each packet. *Good thing you stayed downstairs, and got something done instead, you ninny*, Jane admonished herself with a smile.

Jake went about inspecting the upstairs and found what appeared to be a false wall in the back of the master closet. He told her it was "cobweb city" back there, but that it was a pretty large space, by what he could see. At the mention of webs, Jane knew she would not be exploring that space, until she was certain, all spiders were evicted or relocated, at least. She hated spiders the worst. She could handle most things with ease, but not the spiders.

After a few minutes of looking in the trunk, Jane could sense that Jake was antsy to go back downstairs. She carefully closed the lid on the trunk, and they pushed it back up against the wall. Jake walked out onto the landing and while looking up, he saw the opening to the attic in the corner. Neither had noticed it before.

Jane wondered what other treasures could be up there in the attic. She had not given it much thought before, but if the trunk was here, what else might still be? Her mind raced at the idea. How cool would it be to find more? *Well, enough exploring for one day*, she thought. So they decided to have a sandwich and watch a movie. Jake apparently had this planned all along because he had three movies in the truck. Jane was delighted. She loved it when the man had a plan.

They made popcorn and settled in to watch the DVDs. It turned out that Jake had been most accommodating. He had picked out an old cowboy movie, a recent action movie, and a regular full-blown "chick flick."

Wait a minute, Sally, hold the phone, Jane thought with a chuckle. *This fellow could be a real keeper. He is trying to put his best foot forward, and that is commendable. Actually, it's highly commendable.*

She was not going to rush into anything that was for sure. Time would tell. You couldn't really give up on love, not ever. Somewhere deep down, she realized this. Sometimes you do have to kiss more than one toad to find your prince, maybe even three or four. And she realized that if there was a prince still left out there, she was determined to find him. Life was not meant to be spent solo, anyway. But she was pretty stubborn and set in her ways, at times. She knew that finding a prince to put up with all that she could dish out, could prove quite daunting.

It's the Arrowood way, she reminded herself. Dogged perseverance. That stick-in-there-and-work-it-out kind of pluck was needed, and she knew she had that stuff to spare. *Well. I am pretty much full of it.* And with that thought, she laughed heartily.

"Grandma, what would you think about me up here doing this? Would you be right here beside me, helping if you could? I very much think so," Jane reasoned to herself. "I truly think she would."

With every new project completed, Jane was more and more bolstered with confidence, and more convinced that the house renovations would truly be complete one day.

It would take time, but time was the one thing she had and plenty of it. It was going to be so worth it, she just knew it.

It was soon nearing Valentine's Day, and Jane was looking forward to it for the first time in years. No spending the day avoiding the holiday of hearts for her this year. For the first time in ages, she would finally get to enjoy it.

Jake had told her about how he loved to carve on wood, and he had recently started making wooden walking sticks with carved faces. He was quite skilled at it, and she wanted to find him the perfect Valentine's present, so she ordered him a set of micro carving tools that seemed to be just the thing. She was excited to give him something that he could use. Specialty tools were typically hard to find in the hills, and you usually had to go to a larger city to find something like that. So she felt confident that the gift would please him. She smiled just thinking about it.

The weather was warming up, and so was their relationship. If Jake were growing weary of the time they spent together, she sure couldn't tell it. He seemed to be just as happy and content as she was herself. But knowing what a man was thinking was not Jane's strong suit. She had thought that all was well before, and she could not have been further from the truth, she had to remind herself.

Well, I am going to take each day as it comes and let tomorrow take care of itself, Jane thought. *There's not much I can do besides pray and hope for the best.*

In her Scarlett O'Hara voice, she said, "Tomorrow is another day! Well, I just seem to be getting worse and worse at cracking myself up," Jane chuckled.

The house was finally ready to be painted, and Jane tackled it head-on, with much determination and her own special brand of stubborn. She soon realized that the exterior of the second floor was not even reachable with her ladder. So, she finally gave in after slipping and spilling a gallon of paint and called in a crew to finish the work.

She was glad she had come to her senses and realized that she could not climb a tall ladder and have an epic fail. *Seems I am getting a bit wiser, Dad.* Jane smiled at the thought. *Well, maybe I am, anyway.*

The paint crew talked in loud voices among themselves, right outside the window, after arriving. And then, one by one, they climbed their ladders, and the work commenced in earnest. Jane snuggled into her favorite chair and drank a sip of her freshly made lemonade. Smiling in contentment, she decided that this was the best way to paint the house, after all. She reached for a large packet of the letters that Isabelle had written so long ago. Jane smiled as she slowly untied the faded ribbon that held the precious bundle together.

10

We tell lies when we are afraid…Afraid of what we don't know, afraid of what others will think, afraid of what will be found out about us. But every time we tell a lie, the thing that we fear grows stronger.

~Tad Williams

Nancy's bruises were healing, but they were still very tender to the touch. She was glad that David would not see her at her worst. She saw the rabbit wrapped in burlap cloth, lying on the porch, as soon as she stepped out into the morning light. It must have been too dangerous for him to stay very long. That meant that soldiers were still somewhere near, she reasoned. The lady who lived over in the next hollow had talked to her at length about the dangers of being alone with bushwhackers wandering about.

Nancy had concocted a plausible story about the bruises, saying she had slipped on an icy patch down by the creek. Mountain folk just simply didn't tell everything they knew; they tended to their own business and kept mostly to themselves. That was just the way it was.

Besides, there was nothing that could be done now. What happened had happened. It was done. She was strong, and her baby was

Love and Mercy - Up On Roan Mountain

still lively and kicking. She had noticed no bleeding, and she was healing on the outside. It was the inside that would take time. She cried most nights, but the real pain, deep in her heart, was something she chose to try and keep buried within her.

Telling David about the attack would just never do. He would fly off the handle, sure as the world, and get mad as the devil. He would tear out after the soldiers and wind up getting himself killed. She loved him so and decided that she would never even have to tell him what had happened.

With the rabbit in hand, she went back into the cabin. She had set the pail of water near the fire on the hearth overnight, to keep it from freezing, but she still had to break the ice on the surface of the water before she could use it.

Life on the mountain wasn't easy. The mornings, more often than not, brought a light dusting of snow on the quilts, under which she and the baby slept. She would wake in the morning and take the quilts out to shake off the snow.

This morning she dipped the cloth in the icy water in the bucket and wiped down the table that David had made for her. She loved the golden-colored solid oak planks from which he had hewn their table. He was a fine craftsman. She smiled, thinking of David, and as she wiped, the cloth stuck, frozen to the surface, almost instantly. Her fingertips turned a ghostly pale white from the cold. They stayed cold and white in the wintertime. She tried to warm them by the fire.

She always stoked the fire and added some wood before waking Isabelle. Isabelle slept soundly, still nestled down under the quilts, and Nancy looked at her beautiful daughter with her tousled head of blond curls. She said a silent prayer that God would look after her child, and her David. Little did she know, but at that very moment, David needed all the prayers he could get.

David stood staring at the end of a bayonet that was pointed straight at his heart. The grungy group of men gathered around him, menacingly. David knew that a fight would not end well—they each had quite a few more inches, not to mention more than just a few more pounds, on him. He wouldn't stand much of a chance. But standing before them, he did not allow himself to show any fear, and he knew in his heart he would never back down.

"Just what are you here for?" the largest in the group demanded. "We don't allow any confounded strangers in our camp!"

David swallowed hard and said, "I meant no harm, and I had no way of knowing that I'd entered your camp." He told them that he was simply passing by and thought they may have food, but if not, he would gladly leave them in peace. These types of men were the desperate kind. They were dangerous renegades, no doubt. They were also just as cold, tired, and hungry as David was. They had been forced off their own land and forced into running, and they were not going to be forced into anything else. He could see that in their steely eyes.

11

If you'll go with me to the mountains
And sleep on the leaf carpeted floors
And enjoy the bigness of nature
And the beauty of all out-of-doors,
You will find your troubles all fading
And feel the Creator was not man
That made lovely mountains and forests
Which only a Supreme Power can.
When we trust in the Power above
And with the realm of nature hold fast,
We will have a jewel of great price
To brighten our lives till the last.
For the love of nature is healing,
If we will only give it a try
And our reward will be forthcoming,
If we go deeper than what meets the eye.

~Emma "Grandma" Gatewood

After reading to almost three in the morning, Jane finally stumbled off to bed. Jake was coming early the following day to take her to get more supplies.

She awoke with the sun rising, and she hurriedly showered and made herself presentable. She made some coffee and no sooner than she had poured a cup and taken a sip, Jake knocked on the door.

"The painting is coming along nicely," he said, and then his face slid into a slow wide grin.

She had coffee stains dribbled all the way down the front of her white blouse. She hadn't even noticed. She followed his gaze and her cheeks flushed with embarrassment.

He must think that I can't even drink a cup of coffee without wearing some of it. Nuts. I am continuously looking like a total nutcase to this man, and evidently, I can't even stop myself, Jane lamented to herself. She shrugged her shoulders, smiled good-naturedly, and turned to go back into the bedroom to change her blouse.

Once changed into a fresh blouse, she saw that Jake had found the coffee pot and had poured himself a cup. "Hope you don't mind that I helped myself," he said.

"Not in the least. You know where everything is by now, surely. Besides, it's better that you drink it, than me just wearing it, anyway," she chuckled.

Jake thought, *I could get used to sharing a pot of coffee with this woman. I could get used to it and look forward to it each day.* But he said nothing of the sort; he just smiled at her. Just being with each other was easy, for both of them. *Not a bad thing. Not a bad thing at all,* he thought to himself.

Later, after a full day of running around looking for fixtures, moldings, and receptacles, they were both pretty well tuckered out. The selection in town was not that great, they soon found out, and it was quite a drive to get to a big-box store.

They ate a late lunch and supper combined and enjoyed it immensely.

"Great idea, the barbecue place you suggested," Jane said.

"It was, for sure, the best barbecue I've had since I was last in Lexington, North Carolina. I thought my cousin Mary made the best ribs, but she may have to be relegated to second place after today," Jake said.

"It was really good food," Jane agreed. *And the company wasn't that bad, either*, she thought with a smile.

"I know you are worn out, you have to be," Jake said. "I'm getting pretty tired, myself."

"I want you to know that I appreciate your help today. Your knowledge of building materials and even knowing which way to go, really helped," Jane said, smiling.

He kissed Jane lightly on the forehead and said goodnight. She watched him walk across the porch and down the steps.

Jane slowly closed the door and turned the lock. She stood at the door lost in thought. She stared straight at the closed door, but she did not see it at all. A smile played softly across her face.

Jake walked to his truck not wanting to leave Jane all alone, but knowing that he would. He turned back again, to give the house one last look, and in the window upstairs, movement caught his eye. Standing in the window were two small faces. Two little pale-faced girls were standing side by side, peering down at him. They were hand in hand, with no expression detectable on their faces. He stared up at them for a few seconds, and in an instant, they were gone. Had they really been there? Was *he* seeing things now?

"Maybe I am just more tired than I realize." He chuckled softly to himself. "Well, maybe the house *is* haunted, after all." Then he got in the truck and leaned toward the dash for one more look up at the window, before he put the truck into reverse, backed up, and drove back down the mountain toward home.

Jane watched from the side window until the taillights disappeared into the darkness. *He is something else*, she thought with a smile. She found herself smiling more and more these days. She was happy. *Imagine that. How did that happen?* she mused. She went straight back to the bedroom and opened the old trunk, grabbed a bundle of letters that looked more worn than the others, apparently older. Then she pulled out an old journal. The handwriting inside was fading and spidery, but still legible. Jane changed into her nightshirt and went to the front room, where the lamplight was more suitable for reading.

She read on, completely fascinated, well into the wee hours of the morning. Even then, with her eyes bleary and tired, she did not want to put the journal down.

The handwriting in the journal was slanted, much the same as her own, she mused. *That must be the reason I can read it so easily, it's so familiar to me.*

Isabelle had written down her thoughts and poured her heart into these old crumbling pages, and Jane did not want to miss one single word of it. She devoured it page after page, with hungry eyes. She wanted so badly to finally know the whole story.

12

Your Father knoweth what things you have need of before you ask Him.

~Matthew 6:8

David's eyes were red and sore from little to no sleep in three straight days. The cold had seeped deep into his bones and chilled him to the core. "Being so blame cold at night would probably keep even the devil himself awake," he lamented.

There was no extra flesh on his thin frame to afford him any warmth at all. He was too thin, painfully thin. The words of his father echoed in his mind: "If'n you passed in front of a light, now boy, you'd likely as not see the worms just a workin' and a gnawing away at you." David hung his head.

The men in that camp had finally relented and let David go on his way. He felt that the Lord had watched over him that time, for sure. Next time, he may not be as fortunate. "I need to eat something today. But what will I have for my family? They are hungry, too."

The war was taking a fierce toll on the mountain people. The soldiers took whatever they wanted, leaving the leftovers for the people to survive on, somehow. It was only getting worse, daily, as the fighting continued.

Indians were joining the fight now. There were even rumors that the Indians were scalping the soldiers after they were struck down in battle. Cruel, horrible times were upon them. "God protect us all," David prayed in a whisper. He had heard that further over into Tennessee, jobs were available in the ironworks.

Should he clear out and head for Nashville? The prospect was frightening, but with Nancy pregnant, it seemed near to impossible to get the family safely over the mountain. But work meant food, and food was what they needed most.

David bent over coughing, hard and long. He had been coughing for the past three days. He was getting sicker every day and felt feverish. But he was still determined to try and hunt. Nothing would stop this man who loved his family, nothing at all.

Over in the next valley, there was another small encampment of men. David thought they must be starting camps up here on the mountain for a reason, thinking that they were less likely to be found. They were mostly men that were on the run, and those that did not want to join up with the fighting. Of course, there were others that were just out to steal whatever loot they could come by, taking any opportunity at hand and not caring a bit about the consequences. Walking into another camp could mean certain death, but David was desperate. He was lucky that the first had offered him a bite of food, although begrudgingly, and had then sent him packing.

He decided he would bluff them into thinking that he was one of them. Then he could take any food he could and steal away in the night if he had to. He had to get some food to the cabin, and soon.

Low, rumbling laughter and faint sounds of a guitar being strummed lifted up to where David hid. The camp was down in the gorge below. No fires could be seen, but surely they had some food. He watched from above until he mustered up enough courage to emerge from the shadows and climb down from his perch.

Once out in the clearing, David was soon spotted, and the alarm was sounded. A dove cooed softly up on the ridge above David; then a reply came from down below. David was smart enough to know it was too late in the night to hear a dove call, so he knew instantly that it had to be a signal.

Soon, there were better than ten men standing along the path, right in front of David. David peered anxiously at the dark figures ahead, trying to make out their faces. "Don't mean you no harm, now! Don't mean no harm at all, to you fellers. Just want to come talk with y'uns and see if I could maybe ask you for a bite to eat tonight? Name's David, David Correll."

The silhouetted figures grouped tighter together and the one closest to David was the first to speak. "We don't need no trouble here now, boy. You ain't gonna waltz in here and cause us no trouble. It's just not gonna happen."

"No, sir. No trouble here. I just wanted to ask you for somethin' to eat, I'm mighty hungry," David said. That was certainly no lie. Poor David was so weak from his cough that he was swaying slightly on his feet.

The largest man in the group said aloud, "Aw, now, he looks terribly scrawny to be a causin' us any trouble. Looks like he needs to grab a root, is all." There was scattered laughter among the men. David knew that "grab a root" meant to get something to eat, like a potato. He felt a bit of hope that maybe this would end well, after all.

The last man to speak stepped out of the shadows and extended his huge hand.

"Name's Johnson. I'm the leader of this band of roughnecks. Come on in and grab you a cup of beans and a hoe cake. That's about all we can offer you, but you are more'n welcome to it."

David nodded and shook the extended hand of the man named Johnson. The rest of the men flanked David and escorted him deeper into the woods. David had a fleeting thought that maybe he had just stepped directly into a snare; just like the ones he had built himself, to catch unwary rabbits.

Desperate times can drive a man to do things, things a body would not even consider, normally. These were those desperate times. More desperate than any other time David had seen in his life.

David had no idea of the exact number of men that were in the camp. There were shadows cast all along the ridge, just above the group of rocks, serving as a wind break. It was hard to tell what were just shadows and what were really men.

David offered up his sack of chestnuts that he had tied to his waist. Earlier in the day, he had happened upon a tree with a hollow limb that had been ripped open. Looking into the hole, he quickly determined that it was a ground squirrel's stash of chestnuts. And likely as not, the limb had been torn away by a larger animal, trying to get at the squirrel. There were layers of dirt and chestnuts, just the way a ground squirrel stored them for winter. There were a number of chestnuts scattered about on the ground below. David had quickly gathered them up and placed them in his empty sack.

"Mouse hole hunting," as he had called it when he was a young boy. He and his brothers would go out hunting for squirrels' chestnut stashes quite often.

He had gathered up most of the chestnuts when a sudden high-pitched scream had startled him, and he lost his grip on the sack momentarily. He turned and caught movement above him, and higher up the hill, perched on a rock was a lean panther.

Apparently the panther had his eye on the "mouse hole" as well, and it had torn the branch trying to get inside to the squirrel. David grabbed up the half-full sack and ran. He tripped once but managed to hang on to the sack and most of the chestnuts. He did not stop until he was well out of harm's way, and well out of breath. Panthers, especially hungry ones, were nothing to be reckoned with, and David knew it.

Now, it seemed it was well worth the danger. Having something to offer these men, anything at all, was a bargaining chip, and David felt that it was greatly in his favor.

Several men were preparing some sort of large fire pit and David was aware that many eyes were on him and his every move. He cautiously made no sudden movements and was even more careful to not lock gazes with anyone. Anything could cause them to turn on him, and he surely didn't want to give them a reason, not at all. He was outnumbered in the worst way, and he knew it.

After some time had passed, uneventfully, David began to breathe easier. The others milled around, and he listened as they talked to one another. He stood at a comfortable distance from the other men, keeping mostly to himself. He learned of other nearby renegade encampments much like this one. He learned of deadly encounters with soldiers along the road to Elizabethton. There were occasional crude jokes, some of which David had never heard the likes of. He was a God-fearing man and here, among these bushwhackers, he was surely in a devil's den. It was a testament to the time. *This war is tearing the whole world apart*, David thought. *Nothing will ever be the same as it was before. Men are becoming more and more like wild animals, fiercely protecting what little they have left.*

One man told of the soldiers burning his home. The agony of his loss could be heard in his trembling voice.

"It was the nearest thang to death that I ever did see, watching that house burn. I tell ya it does something to ya, way down inside of ya. It just tears ya up on the inside. It's like death, seeing everything ya got, everything ya worked for, and all the things you treasure, just gone. Why, ya can never replace that. Ya cain't go back. It's all just plain gone, up in the smoke.

"They lit that lamp and tossed it straight through the window at my place. All I could do was watch. They had my girls at knifepoint. There wasn't nothin' I could do. Nothin', but just stand there and watch." Tears streamed down the man's face as he relived the terrible moment. That gut-wrenching moment when his life changed forever was just playing out over and over again, in his mind's eye.

David listened intently, and he slowly realized that these men were just like him, after all. They were just plain mountain folk upon whom the war had come to visit its wrath. No one here had asked for what had happened to them—they were simply caught up in it, trying to stay alive, minute by minute. They were desperate because they were forced into being that way. They had been normal before the war began. War was hell. Plain and simple.

"My Rheda got the typhoid fever and just up and died on me. She was so sick. It was just heartbreakin' to watch. I sent for the doctor to come and look about her, but it was too late. She was just too sick," said the small-statured man. He looked down at his hands as he talked.

"I held her head in my hands, and she looked up at me like she was goin' to try and say somethin' to me, and she just took a little breath and died." He sat with his hands folded neatly in his lap, and he never took his eyes off of them.

Another told the tale of his lost pot.

"We were up crossing the river that day, on our way outta Forsyth County. The Cap'n led us down the river, and we crossed at a shallow ford. Then I saw that my cookin' pot had just fell off somewhere, a ways back. It weren't tied up to my rucksack, where I'd put it. Thought it was surely on there tight enough, but I guess it had worked itself loose. Fell off at the river, I reckon.

"The rest of the company went on ahead, and I circled back for my pot. When I finally found it, ol' Cap'n was nowhere in sight. That's when I seen my chance. Well, I took it. I got on my horse and rode hard, off in the opposite direction. Clear away from that river. Clear away from the army, and clear away from the dang ol' war. I built myself a little shack to hole up in, for the time being. I hunted and fished some. I got by pretty well. It weren't no hard thing to desert the army. Many men had done it before me, and many more done it after I did. I don't regret it. I'd do it all over a'gin. Fighting ain't for me. I jest couldn't do it anymore. No more," he said.

His voice trailed off to barely more than a whisper, and his eyes were focused on the horizon with a blank stare, seeing scenes from his past, and not the horizon at all. The same haunted look loomed in the sunken eyes of many men in the group.

David listened intently with compassion, and then suddenly he saw that there were several hams piled up alongside the fire pit. Hams that were more than likely, taken from local smokehouses by the soldiers. And then stolen from the army and brought here, no doubt.

When the talking tapered off, and the men separated into smaller groups, David saw his chance. He quickly walked over, bent down, grabbed a small ham, tucked it under his loose coat, and made his way quietly out of the camp.

Later, he sliced huge slabs of ham off the bone and crammed them into his mouth. It tasted unbelievably good to the half-starved man. The rest he carefully wrapped back up in cloth. Later, under the cover of darkness, he placed it in a burlap sack and laid it on the corner of the porch, not far from the door. He knew that Nancy would find it, come morning's light.

Standing in the shadows close by the house, he bowed his head to quickly pray. He prayed for an end to this terrible war. He prayed for all the tormented souls back in that camp. He asked that God would watch over his family and protect them, and then he prayed for forgiveness for taking the ham and sent up an honest prayer of thanks to the good Lord for providing it.

Nancy awoke with the baby crying. She felt the child's forehead, touching it with her lips, and it felt almost hot to the touch. She feared it was yet another fever. She tended the fretting child as best she could. She knew she needed to use some of the dried bachelor's buttons that she had harvested and kept from last summer. She went to the wooden box where she stored her herbs and got what she needed.

She always brewed a weak tea with the flowers and added just a touch of honey, so the baby would take it easily. It was as good as she could do for her, in this cold weather. Fresh was always better, but dried was all she had. After letting it steep in the water she'd boiled over the fire, she let the concoction cool somewhat, and then she gave some of it to the feverish baby.

The baby settled down a little after drinking the tea in tiny spoonfuls. Isabelle was soon drifting off to sleep and Nancy pressed her lips to the forehead of the child and smiled in relief. She felt a lot cooler. The fever had broken. She rocked the child in her arms to soothe her and soon fell asleep herself.

There was a sudden noise and then the sound of voices coming from outside, which woke her instantly. She gently laid the baby down and quickly rolled up the blanket and placed it beside her to keep her from rolling off the bed. Nancy went to the window and peeked out. She was careful to stand to the side of the window to lessen the chance of being seen.

Two mounted soldiers were by the path that went from the house down to the creek. She froze in place, terrified. One soldier dismounted, tied his horse to a bush and began walking up the path toward the cabin. The baby awoke, began to fret and then cry out in earnest. Nancy rushed over, picked up the child and placed her hand gently but firmly over the child's mouth, trying to shush her. They stood still and silent, with Nancy listening for the sound of boots thudding on the wooden planks of the porch. She did not have to wait long.

Suddenly, the front door of the cabin flew wide open and slammed against the chair beside it. Two soldiers stood in the doorway; one entered and grabbed at Nancy, but she managed to twist away from the grasp. She recognized him instantly, the same soldier from the creek. He had returned for more of the same; her worst nightmare had come true. The baby was tossed back onto the bed, and when she landed, she screamed out loudly.

Nancy backed away from the child and moved toward the fireplace, hoping to draw the danger away from her defenseless child. A silent scream lodged in her throat, but she would not waste the energy. There was no one to hear it, even if she did. There was no one who could help her now. With her left hand, she felt for the fire poker that she had left propped against the hearth. She found it. Grasping wildly, she grabbed the poker and whipped it out from around her back and brought it crashing down on top of the soldier's head. He never even saw it coming. Blood gushed from the gash across his forehead, and he let out a squeal that sounded more like an animal than a man. The baby screamed and cried and reached out for Nancy.

Stunned, the soldier touched his forehead and saw the blood, which brought instant rage. His brow knit in blind fury. He said not a word but covered the space between Nancy and himself in scant seconds. He grabbed at her but somehow she wrestled herself free once more. Her hand had lost its grip on the poker during the struggle, and it clattered to the floor.

The second soldier had at first stood watch on the porch, but now he entered the cabin. Nancy prayed silently but feared the very worst.

She knew that she had to get to the gun. She'd been terrified to even hold the gun, but now she knew what she had to do. She backed up closer to the fireplace. David had told her that it was there, should she ever need it. She loathed the thought of touching it. She reached out behind her back and tugged the corner of the loose stone right above the fire, out half an inch.

She kept her eyes trained on the soldier closest to her. She held her breath, hoping that the stone would come out easily. It slid soundlessly, and she pushed it over to one side. She had just enough space to place her fingers in the open gap beside it. She whipped around with the gun in her hand as the dislodged stone fell to the wooden floor with a resounding thud. She leveled the double barrels and pointed the gun straight at the soldier. She had barely enough strength in her to hold it out from her body. She trembled fiercely, and the gun barrel trembled as well. She closed her eyes tightly, uttered a barely audible moan, and pulled the trigger. Everything happened in just a few short seconds that sped up and blended into a total blur.

The recoil from the shot flung Nancy back against the hearth, nearly knocking the breath right out of her. The gun's blast was deafeningly loud. The smell of the gunfire was acrid and quickly filled the small cabin with its smoke. The baby wailed on, inconsolably, and the soldier lay decidedly dead, covered in his own spattered blood.

The front of his shirt spread into a deepening red blossom of stain. The gaping hole in his chest, where his heart had been just seconds before sent up a small plume of steam into the cold air of the cabin. The cold was streaming in from the open door. Nancy watched in horrified fascination as the bloodstain slowly spread out, bigger and bigger, on the tattered shirt. It was as if she were outside herself. Somehow, she was just standing there, watching the crimson bloodstain swell, while suspended in time.

She looked up, dazed, expecting to see the second soldier still coming toward her, but he was long gone. The door was swinging on its hinges. As soon as the gun had blasted, he had turned and fled. "Thank you, God, for that," she breathed aloud as her disjointed mind slowly formed the thought.

I have done kilt him, Nancy thought.

A loud sob emitted from her throat. "I raised up that gun and pointed it right at that man's heart and pulled the trigger. I have kilt him, surely kilt him dead. God have mercy on my soul."

She would never have lived through another rape and beating. She knew in her heart and soul that killing a man was against everything she had ever been taught. It was against her Father in heaven, her Lord, against her beliefs, and terribly wrong. "God help me, I have killed him!" Her mind reeled violently from the shock. But somehow, she knew with a deep understanding, that he would have killed her this time, for sure.

The mental anguish would have left her soul dead, and lifeless, even if her body had somehow survived the attack.

Her mind raced with a series of disconnected thoughts. Disbelief. Horror. Unspeakable terror. Then utter shame. All of these disjointed thoughts came racing at her at avalanche speed.

The baby screamed on and on. Overcome with it all, Nancy suddenly crumpled to the floor. With the door wide open and the baby screaming at the top of its lungs, Nancy had passed out cold. The gun clattered to the floor beside her, falling from her limp hand.

Nancy floated away. She dreamed of earlier times when she and David were happy. They were having a midday meal spread out on a blanket in a green grassy meadow, high up on the Roan, filled with wildflowers. The mountain oat grass was thick around them and it swayed in the gentle breeze, sealing off the blanket and transforming it into a small room. The trees stood sentry over them. Nothing was wrong in this world. Nothing could ever hurt them here. The warm sunlight filtered through the trees and lit up the grasses, into a make-believe fairy-tale world.

It was a world where evil did not exist, and pain was not possible. Where men did not rape, and babies did not cry. It was a beautiful world where no one ever went hungry, and no one was ever cold. And Nancy dreamed silently on.

"Isabelle, now hush that crying, baby girl. Momma's here." Smoky, obscure thoughts swirled into the darkness from far away, finally reaching Nancy. She stirred and slowly began to wake, and as she did, her foot moved and touched the leg of the dead soldier. He was lying near her, with thick congealed blood pooled around his body. Raising up, and seeing the leg, she drew her foot back in sudden recoil. Now the baby's screams were hardly discernible above those of Nancy.

Tears poured down her face. With her head resting on her chest, she sobbed aloud, "What am I going to do? How could this have happened? And my baby girl saw it all." She sobbed at the thought. She moved quickly to Isabelle and sheltered her in her arms. The baby was young, so young that her memories would evaporate over time, like a morning's dew, and for that, Nancy was grateful.

She grabbed the blanket off the bed, wrapped it around the baby, and out the open door she fled. She had only one thought, *David*. She knew she had to find David, and find him fast.

She ran to the top of the hillside and tied the red scrap of cloth she had carried in her apron pocket onto the tree branch. She went over to a large rock overhanging the side of the gorge, and she and the baby wrapped up in the blanket, sat under the edge, and waited. The rock afforded some protection from the wind that pummeled the gorge, but precious little. She shivered in the cold, clinging to the baby she held in her arms. "David. Oh, please hurry, please hurry. We need you so, my sweet David."

She fell asleep and woke to her name being called out in the early morning light.

David was alarmed and knew instinctively that something was terribly wrong. He had seen the red cloth after finding the cabin door ajar and came running toward it. David knew that Nancy would never bring the baby out in the cold like this without something being wrong.

He studied her eyes for clues. She burst into fresh tears, and he held her close until she could speak. His heart was breaking at the sight of the bruises that were beginning to heal on her sweet face.

He would kill whoever put those bruises there, he knew that for certain.

She told him all of it, leaving nothing out. He hung his head as tears flowed from his eyes. He held her, touching her face, smoothing her hair, and trying to console her as best he could.

He knew it was all his fault. He should have dug a larger root cellar and hid out there, right beneath the house during the day. He should have stayed close. Close enough to be there to protect his family.

He gathered Nancy and little Isabelle and took the path to his cousin's house on the other side of the Roan. They would both be safe there until he could come fetch them. They all had to get away from this area, and soon.

No one ever missed the renegade soldiers. They were missing when the roll was called in camp, but it was assumed they were still nearby. They had been looking for things to steal and were up to no good when they decided to go back to see if Nancy was still in the little cabin. The one soldier that fled was quickly moving westward and vowed never to return.

Back at the cabin later after darkness had fallen, David wrapped the soldier's lifeless body in an old blanket and struggled to get it out of the cabin. After burying it in the edge of the woods, he finally allowed himself time to rest, but he had little choice at that point. The soldier was head-and-shoulders taller than David, and he was considerably weakened from hunger. David made sure no one saw him. He cleaned the blood off of the floor, replaced the stone, and straightened up the cabin so that no sign of a struggle was evident.

David cleaned the gun, then carefully wrapped it up and pulled out the loose stone in the fireplace by the mantel. He slid the gun back into the small opening. He pushed the stone back into place and knelt beside the fireplace and prayed the most fervent prayer that he had ever prayed in his life. He hoped with all his heart and soul that God had heard his plea and would have mercy on him and his family.

13

It is not the mountain we conquer but ourselves.

~EDMUND HILLARY

NOT KNOWING IF they would ever come back, David took one last look at the tiny cabin, drew a trembling breath, and walked out, closing the door behind him.

He later told his cousin, Vince, that they were leaving for Tennessee in search of work.

The road over the mountain was torturous. They spent far less time traveling each day than David would have liked, but he had a pregnant wife and a baby to consider. The wagon he had borrowed from his cousin was constantly losing the left wheel. He secured it as best he could, and they kept on going. Each new bump from the deep ruts in the road brought Nancy fresh pain, but she endured it all in silence.

Besides her explanation of the events, she had not said anything at all since he had found her huddled under that rock, white as a sheet. He knew that she was not the same smiling girl he had married, and he wondered if she would ever be again. It broke his heart to see her like this. Knowing what that brute had done to her made his clenched fists turn white-knuckled. There was not much he could do about that now, he reasoned. It seemed best to try and forget it for Nancy's sake. But it was just eating away at him to think of a man brutalizing her that way.

The hours stretched into days, and the supply of hardtack and dried meats that his cousin had shared with them was soon growing pretty low. Thank God he had been willing to let them have the meager amount of food that he had. Without it, David knew there was no way they could have survived this trip.

The winding mountain pass had been used for centuries as a trading route by the Indians. The Indians that were left still used it, and they eventually passed a few along the way. Most they encountered were friendly, but a few were menacing, scowling at them as they passed. This caused Nancy much concern. New, unfamiliar land stretched out ahead of David and Nancy, and neither knew what the future held for them.

They found an abandoned cabin near a place called Happy Valley. They decided they would stay there until time to share crop.

It was a quiet little valley, right outside the town of Maryville. Nancy took the name of the settlement as a good sign. *Is it possible to ever be happy again?* Nancy had wondered this time and time again.

Time passed by easily in Happy Valley. It was relatively calm here, but the war still raged on, just outside its perimeter. David and Nancy felt safer here, and they began to try and put the past behind them. Nancy still had a sick dread in the bottom of her stomach at times, especially when soldier troops passed by, but things were some better. She had nightmares occasionally, and she would awaken screaming out in terror, and David would hold her until her crying subsided.

The cold weather passed, and the spring slowly came, then finally the warmth of summer. Little Isabelle was growing fast, with little sister Mary Calla beside her. Mary Calla was born a bit earlier than expected, and terribly underweight, but she managed to survive. Nancy looked at her bright-eyed baby daughter, lying on a blanket in the grass and marveled at her tenacity. She was a little fighter, and she would do just fine in life.

With the warm sunshine on her face, Nancy felt almost content and so much better than she had in a long time. She worked the garden and even helped David till the fields. With each landing of her hoe in the rich dirt, she felt her spirit renewed. "God is good. He has seen us through many troubled times. Thank you, dear Lord, for faithfully watching over us," Nancy whispered in a heartfelt prayer.

David was out in the fields the day the strange man arrived. He rode in on horseback. Nancy walked out onto the porch, wiping her hands on her apron. She shielded her eyes from the morning sun, to see who the rider was. He swung easily off his horse and adjusted his holster, with the gun slung low about his hips. His movement was sure and fluid despite his tall stature. He looked dangerous, with his strong angular jawline and steely eyes, but Nancy raised her chin, determined that no man would ever cause her harm, or fear, not ever again.

The stranger tipped his hat, and his gaze settled on Nancy's face. His eyes immediately softened. She was a beautiful woman, still. *I can see the deep hurt in those blue eyes, but she's still easy to look at*, the man thought.

"Ma'am. Afternoon to you," he said, nodding. "I'm Deputy Marshall Smith, just come over the mountain, from Mitchell County over in North Carolina. I'm here on official business. I come to ask your husband about a soldier man that was kilt, up on Roan Mountain. Might'n your husband be somewhere about this morning?"

Nancy went instantly weak in the legs. Her throat tightened. She felt as if a heavy vise had clamped down hard, twisting its weight sharply onto her stomach.

They had finally come for her. Surely this deputy knew what she had done. He could see the guilt on her face—it must be as plain as day. She felt as if she could not focus, almost like she was about to pass out. She steeled herself against the feeling of her legs going out from under her.

She thought about her precious daughters and with all the grit she could muster, she somehow found her voice. She stammered at first, then, more clearly, she said, "My, my husband's out in the field, working."

Deputy Smith nodded and turned to look out over the plowed field to the left of the cabin and scanned the horizon for David.

Seeing no one, he turned back to Nancy and asked, "Might I get some water for my horse and a swallow or two for myself?"

Nancy obliged. Carrying the water pail over to the well, and dropping it in, she carefully lowered the bucket for the deputy. While she peered over into the well, the bucket lowered slowly down.

A shaft of sunlight through the clouds illuminated the water below, briefly, and Nancy could have sworn she saw the face of the dead soldier swirling on the reflective surface. In that glimpse, she saw his face twisted into a horrible death mask, his lips snarling up at her.

Nancy gasped. It was as if he had been standing right beside her and looking down into the water.

Nancy's horrified gasp went unnoticed by the deputy; he was busy beating the dust off his road-grimy clothing with his hat. She said a silent prayer in thanks as she quickly lowered her gaze away from the deputy.

Taking a shaky breath for courage, she slowly turned and offered the water to the deputy. "My husband more than likely won't quit working the fields until closer on to suppertime," Nancy told the deputy with a thin smile pasted onto her face. "You are more than welcome to wait for him," she said with a lowered gaze.

Deputy Smith absently rubbed the beard stubble on his chin as he carefully studied Nancy's face. After a moment, he determined that he would ride on into Maryville and get himself a bath and a decent bed for the night, before meeting back up with David.

Besides, the only thing that tied this couple to the dead soldier was the fact that he was figured to have been murdered in the vicinity of a cabin they once lived in, the seasoned deputy thought. The neighbors had told him they had long since moved on, months before the soldier's shallow grave had been found after having been dug up by a pack of dogs. The deputy felt there was no immediate rush to talk to David, with not much more than that to go on, and especially since he now knew where he lived.

Nancy swallowed hard, fighting the urge to be sick. She watched the deputy mount his horse, tip his hat, and then ride away in a cloud of dust.

He knows what happened. He knows it all, she thought in terror. She felt positively ill. She turned and stumbled, almost losing her balance on shock-weakened limbs. She steadied herself on the porch post and leaned hard against the railing, afraid she would faint.

She considered for a brief moment calling out to the deputy, to stop him and confess her horrible deed, and just get it over and done with. Then she remembered her two little girls. They needed her. She was sure she would never be free of that horrible day.

David was not a dishonest man; he simply did not have it in him. He was a God-fearing man, a good man. Now, she had killed that soldier, and there was no turning back the hands of time. The deed was done, and her fate was sealed. David would have no choice but to tell the deputy the truth about what had happened.

Nancy had thought long and hard before David returned from the plowing that day. She had devised a plan where she would parcel out the girls. Mrs. Henley was a good woman and would do right by her girls. David could still see them whenever he wanted. The girls would not have to bear the weight of their momma's shame. No one would expect David to raise the girls alone. He could remarry and make a new family for himself, a new life.

She would just confess and get it over with and behind her. No more running or looking over their shoulders in fear. It was all just more than Nancy could bear. She was about to write out her letter explaining it all when David burst in the door.

Love and Mercy - Up On Roan Mountain

"I saw him. He's come for us, ain't he?" David blurted out as he ran into the cabin.

Nancy looked up at him with eyes crimson from crying and said, "Yes, he's come for me, not us." "I've done the crime, and I will be the one who pays for it." "That man died because of me."

"I will never let him take you from me, Nancy. He will have to kill me first," David said with clear conviction. He had never meant anything more in his life.

Later that night, after waiting until everyone was deeply asleep, David packed his few clothes together in a bundle, along with a few cold biscuits, some jerky, and some hardtack. He gingerly kissed the forehead of his sleeping girls and wife and headed out of the cabin and out of Happy Valley.

He rode into Maryville and asked around for the name of the hotel where the deputy was staying. After finding it, he paused at the bottom of the stairs only briefly before he went up to the room and knocked on the door.

A still half-asleep deputy squinted in the dim light of the hallway when he opened his door.

David confessed to the killing. David told Deputy Smith that he had entered the cabin while the soldier was attacking his wife, and he had shot him dead. He explained it with short, blunt sentences, in pure mountain fashion. The deputy readily believed him guilty; he had no real reason not to. He took David straight to the Maryville jail and locked him in.

David soon learned that Henry Mack Pruett was the name of the man who had cruelly raped his Nancy. He also found out that Pruett was from Virginia. The jail cell doors clanged loudly as they shut behind him, and David hung his head. He knew in his heart he would never see his family again, but he wouldn't have wanted to live another day if they had come and taken his Nancy. It was dark and cold in that jail cell, and as the long hours of the night passed, slowly David realized the depth of the predicament he found himself in.

Killing a man in a crime of passion could easily get you the noose. The deputy thought for sure that David was a deserter and had killed to avoid being caught. David quietly accepted his fate and prayed that God would protect his girls.

No thought was given to the fact that the soldier had been shot in the chest, and David had given his account of coming in and shooting him in the back. The details didn't matter that much to the deputy—his job was done, as far as he was concerned. He had a confession, after all. Deputy Smith was an honest man, just eager to get home and back to his own bed.

Early the next morning, the deputy came and got David, to start on the long ride back to Mitchell County.

Word spread quickly of David's arrest in the tiny community, but no one could believe that David had killed anyone. At least, not until they had heard that he had confessed to the crime. Rumors were quickly spread about what was to happen to Nancy and the girls.

Whispers and idle talk were found in every little town, especially when there was nothing much else to talk about. They quickly labeled him a coward for shooting the soldier in the back. The soldier was only doing his duty, coming to arrest and take back a worthless deserter.

Nancy sat on the bed, staring blankly out the window of the tiny cabin. Her baby, crying and hungry, was wrapped up in a small bundle and lay on the bed beside her. Isabelle sat on the floor, playing with blocks, occasionally looking up at Nancy. But Nancy didn't hear the baby's plaintive cries. She sat looking out, with little expression in her eyes at all.

Her life would never be the same.

The trial was short, and they locked David away, preparing for the hanging. The Roan straddled the Tennessee and North Carolina state lines, but the murder had happened in Tennessee, so the hanging would take place over the line in Tennessee. With the war going on, Mitchell County had the only available deputy to send out to investigate the murder, so Deputy Smith had gone, begrudgingly.

Carter County was nearly a hundred and sixty miles of rough mountain terrain away from Happy Valley, and much too dangerous a journey for a slip of a girl and two young children to make alone. She knew that she would never see her David again. It broke Nancy's heart completely.

The townsfolk talked among themselves, and the consensus was that it was "just as well" that she never would get to see him again. They didn't understand the strong bond that existed between them. Faced with a lifetime without David, Nancy felt her heart had been ripped right out of her. They reasoned that she was young and pretty, and would soon find another and marry.

Talk among the locals was harsh when it came to the opinion of David. He was labeled a "yellow-bellied coward" from the moment he was arrested, and no one cared much about the truth. The rumors went around and around, and with each telling, the story became more and more sordid. The only thing that stayed the same was the label of 'coward'. That stuck, for sure. And as people tend to do, they delighted in the retelling of the juicy story, of the "horrible murdering of a fine upstanding soldier by a cowardly, good-for-nothing deserter."

Life resumed after they hung her David, but just on the surface for Nancy. She was just a shell of her former self. She raised her girls as best she could, and struggling to keep food on the table became a way of life of her.

She solemnly accepted it. She never spoke of David again. She sat in silence most of the time, staring out at nothing, suffering from the loss of her one true love.

A cold, lifeless look slowly crept in to replace the vibrant light that was once in her eyes. Like a summer sun struggling to shine through darkened rain clouds, Nancy's sparkle was now hidden forever behind thick dark clouds of sorrow.

Dreams of that horrible day haunted even poor Nancy's sleep. She would awaken bathed in sweat, always to look down at her hands, seeing them still covered in blood. The horror of the moment never left her. The invisible bloodstains were still very visible to her, long after she had scrubbed her hands raw.

Knowing that David had willingly taken her blame, and saved her, broke her spirit over and over again, as the years tumbled by, one by one. She didn't believe that she deserved to live, yet live she did.

Isabelle eventually assumed the role of mother to her younger sister. She braided her hair and tended to her in every way that her mother simply could not. Isabelle was the one that Mary Calla turned to when she needed anything. Nancy tried to be there for her daughters, but as they grew, she became more and more distant. She would sit for hours staring at nothing. Sometimes grief can kill you just as dead as a bullet can or a rope. She could not let herself forget, and it eventually took her mind, long before it took her body.

Isabelle tended to her younger sister and the vegetable garden. She went to town to get the supplies they needed. She made sure Nancy bathed and changed her clothes. She made sure Nancy ate enough. The days were long for Isabelle, but she loved her mother, and she tried to understand what was hurting her so badly.

Isabelle grew into a beautiful girl herself, but she never saw it. She went over to John Garland's house, over on the next farm, to give his eldest daughter the lace she had crocheted with the finest of stitches with simple cotton thread. She wanted to offer it to her for her wedding dress that was being made. Isabelle did fine, intricate work, admired by many of the ladies at church.

The wedding was set for three months away when the circuit preacher was scheduled to preach in their community.

"Why are you always so kind to me, Isabelle? You must surely be an angel sent down from heaven," a thrilled Emily Garland marveled. "I am sure this will be the most beautiful wedding dress that Happy Valley has ever seen!"

Isabelle looked down at her worn shoes, embarrassed and more than a little surprised at the compliment. She felt it was just the right thing to do, to give the lace to Emily. Emily was not the most well-liked person in town, but Isabelle knew that no one else was going to offer her any help. She had earned a reputation as being a bit uppity, and she did tend to look down her nose at most everyone. But Isabelle knew that down deep, Emily was just a self-conscious, sad-hearted girl. She had lost her mother just last summer and had no one to help her sew her wedding dress. Isabelle's beautiful lacework would make any sewing look better, so she knew it was only right to help her.

Emily held up the lace to admire it in the sunlight streaming through the window. "Why, this is just almost as pretty as the store-bought lace I looked at last week in Maryville."

Just almost, Isabelle thought, disheartened. *It's only almost as pretty.*

Isabelle took a deep breath and realized that was the closest she was going to get to a proper thank-you. She tried to contain her hurt feelings and smiled broadly. She then offered Emily her best wishes on her upcoming wedding. Isabelle said her good-byes and made her way out past the hay barn toward home.

There was a clatter of noise coming from the barn and Isabelle turned to look, shielding her eyes from the bright sunlight. Suddenly, there appeared a tall boy with jet-black hair standing up in the barn's loft. He was wearing dungarees with no shirt. He was muscular and tanned, leaning on a pitchfork, taking a break from his work. He was just standing there, staring down at Isabelle, smiling. Isabelle looked up and thought how white his teeth looked against his tanned skin. *My, how handsome he is*, she thought with a shy smile. Isabelle looked down and away quickly. *He must be the new hand I heard them talking about hiring.*

"Hello! Name's Welzia Arrowood. What might be your name, pretty lady?" he called down to her, but Isabelle hurried on home. *Mother will be needing her supper soon.* Worried that maybe she had been gone too long already, she broke into a full run. Welzia watched her run, smiling after her.

Once back home, she saw that Mary Calla had already started setting the table and had a stew boiling away in the kettle. Isabelle was so proud of Mary Calla and grateful for her help. She would make a fine lady one day.

Nancy sat in the rocking chair. Rocking slowly back and forth, staring straight ahead but seeing nothing.

She murmured occasionally and moved her lips as if she were talking to someone. Her eyes were always so sad and forlorn. When she stared out at nothing like this, it made Isabelle worry. The look in her mother's eyes made Isabelle so upset that she was sick to her stomach. No one should have to suffer so. It was terrible, seeing her mother like this. She remembered the strong, proud woman she once was and seeing the tortured soul she had become, terrified Isabelle.

Nancy was murmuring even louder, rocking back and forth continuously. Sometimes, Isabelle wanted to scream at her, to shake her and tell her to come back to her, to come back to them. All she wanted was for her to be their mother, as she once was. But try as she did, Isabelle could not reach Nancy. Isabelle was so ashamed of herself at times, for being so selfish.

At least she knew that wherever her mother's mind was, she was not suffering, not as she would be back in reality. She had a full heart of compassion for her, but some days it was just too painful to watch. Sometimes in her dreams, her mother was better, but deep down in her heart Isabelle knew it would never be.

Nancy thought back to earlier days as she rocked slowly back and forth. Being a coward and a deserter carried more shame in the eyes of the locals than killing someone outright ever could. Not standing up and fighting for your country, why it was a sin against them all. Nancy wanted to shout out the truth, but she did not dare. If they took her away, what would become of her beautiful daughters? So she suffered on in silence. The years passed, and slowly but surely, the loss drained the very life out of her. Time slowly killed her, just as surely as if the noose had been put around her neck, as well. She prayed that God had shown her David mercy in the end. Her love was labeled a coward, and he was the bravest man she had ever known.

Not very long after seeing her on the Garlands' farm, Welzia began to court Isabelle in earnest, bringing her flowers and tokens of his love. She finally accepted his arm at the church socials, and eventually they were considered an item. Welzia did not have much in the way of worldly goods. His father, Samuel, had died when he was just a young boy, and his stepfather had children of his own, so he stood to inherit nothing. But that did not matter much to Isabelle.

Isabelle knew he was a good man with a good heart, destined to become a preacher, as many in his family had been before him. She loved him dearly, and he loved her, and that was the only thing that mattered to her.

Isabelle happily accepted Welzia's proposal of marriage, and they married on a sunny day in April.

The little family lived together after Isabelle and Welzia wed. But, Mary Calla had her own private dreams and aspirations, too. She was a quite handsome girl with eyes that always seemed to be focusing on things that were far away. She always looked to the horizon, as if she longed to be somewhere else. Even while working in the garden, pulling weeds from around the beans, Mary Calla kept her eyes fixed on the distant hills. She was always looking for someone or something to come and take her away to another place, and to her destiny.

Mary Calla had always felt an unnamed and indescribable loss deep within her. A deep longing for something whose identity continually escaped her. She could never talk about it with anyone, and she never really understood it. But it was always there. She was a lonely soul. Even in the midst of others, Mary Calla felt alone. She felt as if she was mourning the loss of something, continually, and she had no idea why. Her days were filled with pondering this and her nights were filled with vivid dreams. Not horrible dreams, but more like warm memories. Memories of a past she, herself, had never experienced.

Mary Calla never knew why she had these recurring dreams. But there was a reason for it all. She had been born a twin. Her identical twin sister had died at birth and Mary Calla had never been told.

Nancy and David never talked to each other about the second baby girl born that day. Some things were just too painful. Nancy wrapped the still baby, lovingly, in a hand-stitched blanket and finally kissed the child on the forehead with tears streaming down her face. She prayed for angels to come and see the baby girl safely home to heaven. David took the baby, his own tears coursing down his face, and buried the tiny bundle out by a lonesome pine, about two hundred feet or so away from their cabin, in Happy Valley. Nancy wanted her buried close by, in sight of the cabin.

Nancy had held those babies to her chest, one in each arm, for nearly a full day before finally handing the dead child over to David. She was just unable to accept that the baby had never taken its first breath. Devastated by the loss of the tiny sweet-faced girl, Nancy never spoke of her again.

Mary Calla never knew the reason, but her constant scanning of the horizon was just a futile attempt to find her missing twin and feeling that constant loss. She was unknowingly searching for a face very much like her own, a face that she was never able to find.

Isabelle reckoned that you were never closer to another human being as you were with your twin in the womb. Sharing your entrance into the world, from the very first moment, is an experience like no other. The sharing of the first ever touch. Closeness like that can never be duplicated.

Some say that one twin can feel what the other twin is experiencing. Isabelle concluded that maybe Mary Calla even felt her own twin's death state.

Mary Calla was cold yet again. Cold to the core and the sun was shining brightly today. She shook her head, wondering. She tugged her shawl tighter around her thin shoulders, and then Mary Calla gripped the handle of the bucket and toted the heavy water back up to the cabin.

"I must be getting sick," Mary Calla concluded to herself. "This cold feeling must be a fever, and it's just a-coming on, lightning fast. My hands and feet are always so cold," she said under her breath. Isabelle was peeling potatoes seated at the table, and she looked up when Mary Calla entered the cabin.

"How come you are so cold? It's nice outside today, and at least that terrible wind has quit a-blowing so hard. It nearly blew the shutter off the house on the north side yesterday."

Mary Calla shivered again and shook her head once more. "I don't know, it's just me, I guess." Mary Calla looked down at her fingertips, and they had turned a pale ghostly shade once again.

Isabelle looked up at Mary Calla with eyes brimming with compassion. She remembered what the old folks in town had always said: "Twins remember." Isabelle had always known about the twin. She was little at the time, but she remembered. Isabelle had never spoken of it to Mary Calla because intuitively she knew that some things were just too painful to talk about. Her mother was pained enough in her short life. She knew that a body has a limit to what it can endure, and her poor mother had reached her breaking point. She saw her mother's haunted eyes whenever she closed her own. But Isabelle was sure she knew why her sister felt so cold. She felt what her tiny twin felt as it lay in the cold ground.

Isabelle remembered all that had happened; she remembered it well. But she felt certain, deep down in her heart, that Mary Calla need never know.

Their beloved mother, Nancy, passed away that year, easily and silently in her sleep. She just drifted away. Isabelle and Mary Calla both deeply grieved the loss, but each knew she was finally at peace. They buried her on the knoll in the tiny cemetery overlooking the valley in a beautiful place. She was wearing her finest dress with wildflowers lovingly woven into her hair. Welzia moved the baby girl's remains to the cemetery as well, at Isabelle's request, knowing that Nancy would have wanted her baby girl nearby.

Mary Calla was sickly and frail. She would take on a racking cough and keep it for what seemed like months. She had a constant paleness in her face that was especially worrisome to Isabelle.

That following year, several locals and farm hands came to help Isabelle and Welzia bring in the corn crop. Several families banded together when it was time to bring in the crop, calling it a "shucking." It provided a quick and much easier way for each farmer to harvest the corn, and it was also a much-anticipated social event.

Anytime the mountain people gathered it was a celebrated event. Sheets and blankets were spread on the ground for picnics, and young girls and boys got a chance to socialize in Happy Valley. Smiling faces were seen all around as they shucked the corn and piled it up in huge stacks. The laughter, music, and dancing went well into the night.

Isabelle lost sight of Mary Calla in the group of people standing around, and when she did finally find her, she was sitting on a bale of hay. She had found a nice spot in the shadow of a large tree, out of the hot sun. She was seated by the barn with a certain young man from a few farms down the road named William Garland.

Love and Mercy - Up On Roan Mountain

William was a nice young man that Isabelle liked quite a lot. Mary Calla had her head bent down in shyness as William talked to her, but Isabelle could tell Mary Calla was smiling. It was a rare event to see Mary Calla smiling so.

This lifted Isabelle's spirits, and she said a silent prayer that this match would be made. It had to be a true blessing from God. William Garland would be able to provide Mary Calla with a good life, maybe even true happiness and this thought caused Isabelle to smile broadly, herself.

"Now, William, you are embarrassing me with such talk," giggled Mary Calla with flushed cheeks. "Why, my goodness, we just met."

"Don't matter at all, Mary Calla. Love wants what love wants," William said dramatically in his slow drawl, "and I want you. We can marry up in the fall, and then I can get started on our house. My father gave me a piece of land just north of our farm, and I think it will make us a right good little home. Imagine that, Mary Calla, a farm of our very own. We can have chickens and cows and whatever your heart wants. I will work hard, and we will have more than enough, Calla, I promise you. Just say you will, please? I will now, I honestly will. I will work hard to make a home for us, and you will have a happy life with me, I swear it," William said with his jaw set in determination.

Mary Calla laughed out loud at his serious expression, and it caused poor William to turn beet red. She instantly felt bad for him. "Now, William, please don't take on so. I reckon we can start courting and getting to know one another, and then, after a while, I can give you my decision. But not in one day! What will the neighbors think about such a thing?" Mary Calla said with a chuckle. "Meeting one day and married the next? Why, it's not done, Mr. Garland, it's just simply not done. You can court me good and proper, and we can get to know one another, and after time goes on, then we will see."

William's color slowly faded to a lesser shade of red, and he took off his straw hat and wiped his perspiring brow with his hanky.

"Well," he softly chuckled, "I reckon I did let myself get a little ahead of it all, that time. I just saw you standing there and saw how truly purty you are, and I pert near lost my head. I know you're right. And rightly and proper like, I do intend to court you until you say you will marry me. We was just meant to be together; I knew it the moment I laid eyes on you. You mark my words, Miss Mary Calla Correll, we are gonna be man and wife one day, and soon!" William drawled. In his honest twang and countrified manner of speech, young William had endeared himself to Mary Calla almost instantly.

She found herself lost again, deep in her thoughts, just a few moments later, and she cast a mournful glance out over the field of cornstalks. William saw her look and the dark shadow that fell over her face as she looked past him toward the horizon. He felt instant sorrow for this beautiful girl, and he made a promise to himself that he would make her happy. With everything he had inside him, he vowed to spend his life making Mary Calla happy.

She felt vaguely that the missing factor in her life was somehow her fault. She felt sure she was at fault for something that was just terrible, but what?

She had no way of knowing that her own movement in her mother's womb had caused the umbilical cord to wind around the throat of her tiny sister, slowly squeezing the life out of her. She only felt the strangely elusive sense of guilt that was constantly with her.

Woven together inside her was all the guilt of living, while her twin did not. Breathing in the fresh air, smelling fresh meadow grasses, and feeling the warmth of the sun on her skin, and all the while, her twin, her other half, could not. Not knowing why she felt this way was slow torture to Mary Calla.

Mary Calla and William Garland courted for a proper time and then they were married. The wedding came that following spring. The bride wore her best dress and Isabelle wove a delicate wreath of lily of the valley flowers into her hair. She was happy, finally. She felt a strange calming peace on the day of her wedding. She marveled at the feeling. She had no pain, no guilt, and no negative feelings. She swirled in front of Isabelle in her dress and laughed as a young bride should.

Isabelle held back stinging tears looking at dear Mary Calla. She reached up and tucked another lily of the valley into her headpiece. They stood looking at each other for a moment. Smiling through her tears, Isabelle held Mary Calla's hand and told her that she was so very proud of her.

"You're the spitting image of Mother. Momma and Daddy both would be ever so proud, if they could only see you now."

Mary Calla smiled as a tear rolled down her cheek. She absently wiped it away. "No tears today," Isabelle admonished, laughing. "No tears will rain on this happy day."

Outside in the sun, the townspeople had gathered to watch the young couple join.

Wagons were pulled all along the sides of the fields, and many had traveled quite a distance. The word spread quickly, and a chance to celebrate and play music was welcomed by all. Life was not easy in these mountains, but at times it could be very rewarding.

The winds blew gently into the valley, and the grasses swayed in the sun. The music from the fiddle players wafted up and over the pines that bordered the plowed fields. Laughter and revelry echoed down over the valley until the wee hours of the morning. It was a grand wedding, one that was remembered for a long time afterward.

The bride smiled a smile that none could compare to, as she happily kissed her new husband.

They built a little house on the land given to William by his father. They had the chickens and the cows they had spoke of and even a couple of goats, eventually. She had all that she had always dreamed of, and it simply delighted Mary Calla.

Life passed quickly, as life tends to do, and soon the first baby arrived. William and Mary Calla named the baby girl Ollie. A few years passed, and they had two more daughters. Little Minnie was born and soon after, little Ruby. Life together was good for William and Calla. They loved one another deeply as they spent the years tending the small farm, planting their crops, and harvesting them. As the years passed, Mary Calla learned to deal with her depression, and she tried her best to get on with the act of living.

Mary Calla woke one morning in the early light, feeling ill. She became dreadfully sick to her stomach later that morning, and violently so. William came back in from the fields several times during the day, just to check on her. He had worried all the time he was away from her.

Mary Calla wondered to herself if she could be with child. She was totally convinced of it about a week later. She had begun to think her family was complete, but now she had happy thoughts of giving William a son. Finally, he would have the son he so badly wanted. He had never come right out and told her this, but she knew. He wanted someone he could teach to hunt and farm, and all the things that men do with sons. This time, tears of joy rolled down Mary Calla's face.

These same tears of joy soon turned to agony. When she was just about five months along in the pregnancy, she heard the terrified screams echoing from down by the creek and knew in her heart that death had come to Happy Valley.

Losing Minnie and Ruby was the final blow that erased her will to live. Mary Calla collapsed and never recovered. She went into premature labor, and the tiny boy child was born, and then the life slowly ebbed away from Mary Calla, along with her life's blood.

With the sheets drenched and Mary Calla lying lifeless, her eyes stared out unseeing, still showing her intense pain, even in death. William was a broken man from that very moment until the end of his life. He tried, but he was never really able to be a father to the boy, the son that he had so wanted. Every time he looked on the face of this innocent child, he saw the pale death mask of his beloved Calla. She was dead, all because of the boy. He never was able to call him "William." Instead he called him simply, "the boy." The tiny boy baby lived, despite the tremendous odds stacked against him.

Knowing how he felt about William Jr. would have broken poor Mary Calla's heart. Having little supervision from his father, William grew up wild and free, roaming the hills of Tennessee. Even as a young teen, he was gone most of the time, only occasionally returning to Happy Valley. William felt so disconnected from his family that he soon disconnected from everything.

William Jr. became well known in the Valley and even beyond and into eastern Tennessee.

"Wild Bill," as he became to be known, was infamous for his numerous exploits and run-ins with the law. He felt no connection to his father or the rest of the Garland clan, as they soon had nothing to do with him. He was heard to say often, "I'm the son of a pistol, so I'm just one mean son of a gun." Not many would argue that statement. So eventually he changed his name to Correll, his mother's maiden name, and was known by that for the rest of his days.

Changing your name was simple then—you just used the name you wanted to use. No documents were needed. You simply called yourself what you wanted people to call you, and it was so.

He felt a connection to the Correll name and bore it proudly. Wild Bill roamed the countryside and when he saw someone who was going without, he would find someone who had plenty, take from them, and give it to those in need.

The wealthier families of the mountain area of East Tennessee cried out for help from the local authorities, but to little avail. Wild Bill would work under cover of darkness and the people who did notice his taking simply chose to look the other way. Poor was poor then, even worse than it is now, and there were plenty who lived without enough to eat way up in those mountains. Among the poorest, Wild Bill was seen as a hero for the kindness he showed them. A basket full of eggs would appear on the front porch just when it was needed the most, and a cow would be found tied up in the barn, just when the sickly new baby needed milk.

They appreciated the help and were grateful. Many family legends were told and retold in the coming years about Wild Bill, and eventually the thin line that separates fact and fiction became permanently blurred. All legends come into existence by stories being told and retold down through the years, and more often than not, most legends do have more than a grain of truth in them.

Wild Bill died in his early forties, without ever knowing that his mother had been pregnant with two babies when he was born. His twin did not survive the birth. One could reason that he felt his wanderlust and constant restlessness because his "other half" was dead. This loss may have brought him the same torment that his mother had experienced in life, but you can never really know for sure. Did the loss of his twin cause him to be wild, or was it just his nature? Only the poor soul who lived it knew for sure.

Up on a hill, overlooking Happy Valley, lies a tiny cemetery. The Correll family is buried here, alongside the Arrowoods. Two families joined forever. Birds chirp merrily, tiny butterflies flutter in the warm summertime meadow below, and eventually the cool fall breeze blows the dried, fallen leaves across the browned grass and they scatter into a hundred or so different directions. They scatter just as the winds of time have scattered the descendants from these people away from the place that they once knew as home.

Isabelle was terribly sad in Happy Valley. Even the name of the community was a taunt, in light of everything that had happened. Calla was just too young to have died, and it was still so hard to accept it. Isabelle felt misery here; she felt she could not escape the tight hold it had on her fragile heart. Her mother's grave was in that small cemetery, with Calla and her tiny twin buried nearby. She went almost daily to place fresh wildflowers on the graves. It was sad to see how fast the flowers wilted, and Isabelle sank deeper and deeper into a dark depression.

She just wanted to go home. Welzia wanted his wife to be happy. He could see how tormented she was. So together they decided

Love and Mercy - Up On Roan Mountain

to head for the Roan. Loading up what they owned on the wagon, and hitching the two remaining goats to it, they started the hard journey of more than a hundred and sixty miles over mountainous terrain.

It meant treacherous paths had to be navigated. They were jostled over each wagon-wheel rut until their very bones ached from it. They stopped for breaks quite often, and after weeks of weary travel, they were finally there.

The Roan was a blue hazy mist looming on the horizon and to Isabelle it had never been lovelier. She felt her heart lighten at the sight, but when they were finally at the cabin all the memories of sadness here came washing back over her. She sat in the wagon and cried. She had felt that somehow she had left the misery behind her, and the realization that she hadn't was heartbreaking.

Welzia was quite bewildered, and he tried his best to comfort her, but he had no way of knowing just how deeply this hurt went for Isabelle. Her mother's torment was seemingly endless in her short life, and now with dear, sweet Calla gone, she needed a fresh start. She knew this as surely as she knew anything. Isabelle was determined to make that fresh start, so she tried just to cry it all out.

If she stayed mired in the past, she would never be the wife that Welzia deserved. "Kind, sweet Welzia." She smiled through her tears. He always tried his best to be a good husband. He deserved a good wife. She vowed to take care of him and make a family. A family of their own, just like Welzia had always wanted. It would be here. It had to be here. Here in this cabin, where she had been brought into the world. This would be the needed fresh start for them both. She had asked God to help her, and she felt sure He had heard her prayers.

The cabin was in bad shape, but through Isabelle's eyes it was perfect. Welzia saw it quite differently. He saw the sagging roof, and all the repairs that were sorely needed, and his shoulders slumped at the amount work that lay stretched out before him. He took a deep, ragged breath and said a silent prayer. *No sense in lamenting this now—daylight's a-wasting*, thought a determined Welzia.

He unhitched the horses from the wagon, untied the goats, stepped up onto a wheel hub, and pulled down a kerosene lamp that hung from the post of the wagon. He jumped down, struck a match on the sole of his dusty boot, and lit the lamp. The evening was coming on fast, and the dwindling sunlight was casting deep shadows through the thick trees surrounding the cabin.

He wanted to check on what may be in the cabin before Isabelle went inside. Cougars and bobcats had been known to wander these hills, and even raccoons could be nasty mean, as well. *Any ol' varmint could have made its home inside that cabin, with the door standing ajar*, Welzia thought.

Once on the porch, Welzia was relieved to see that the boards looked solid enough. The third step had given way and crumbled beneath his weight—the wood was completely gone—but that much he had fully expected.

Crossing the threshold and into the cabin, the lamplight showed nothing inside at first, besides a small cot pushed up against the wall and a bucket sitting on the hearth.

With a piercing scream exploding in his ears, Welzia raised his free arm to protect himself as a bobcat suddenly pounced down from the rafters of the cabin. He reeled off to one side, still hanging onto the lamp that was swinging wildly and casting crazy shadows all over the cabin's walls.

Choking back a scream of his own, Welzia swung at the bobcat with the lamp. The lamp went flying, slapping against the wall of the cabin with a clatter, and then it burst into sudden flames. The bobcat was hit a glancing blow, but the burst of flames was more than enough to cause it to flee.

Welzia stood dazed momentarily, and then he sprang into motion to douse the flames. He grabbed up an old blanket that was hanging in tatters, from the bed and smothered the flames as best he could.

Hearing the cat's scream, Isabelle came running full speed, up the path from the wagon. In that instant, the bobcat flew out the door and went flying past her on the path. Without giving her own safety a second thought, Isabelle ran straight through the open door of the cabin. She was intent on seeing that her Welzia was all right. The bond of love between them was strong and undeniable.

Isabelle instantly saw the angry blister beginning to form on Welzia's hand, and she moved quickly to help. Grabbing the bucket on the hearth, she ran down to the creek to get cool water for his burned hand.

Only allowing himself a manly wince, Welzia lowered his burned hand slowly into the cool water. Satisfied that Welzia would be alright, and very thankful that the cat had not done more harm than it had, Isabelle swept out the cobwebs in the cabin. Then she brought in their feather ticking, to put on the cot for the night. Too tired to worry about leaving most of their belongings on the wagon, they curled up together on the tiny bed and slept soundly.

Nearing daylight, Isabelle awoke with a start. Thinking that the cat was back, she sat up halfway, pushing Welzia's arm away from her waist, alarmed. She could see nothing moving in the cabin. There was only dark stillness, with no discernible movement outside. She slowly sank back into the soft feather tick and allowed herself to take a deep breath.

We are finally home. This is where I belong, and this is where I shall stay. The Roan has been whispering to me all these years. It has kept calling me, telling me to come on back. Welzia and I will make our home here and hopefully, God will bless me with children finally, and we will raise our family right here on the Roan. The mountain wants me here; I am certain of it. It will supply us with all we need, Isabelle thought with a deep sigh of relief. Unknown to Isabelle, her thoughts echoed the words of her mother, spoken decades before.

Isabelle lay still on the bed as dawn slowly came. She asked God to allow peace to find them here on the Roan. A fire in the fireplace was a comforting thought, so she slipped out of bed to start one. She soon stoked the flames, warming the cabin before Welzia awoke. As she sat on the hearth, she watched the flames flicker. Her mind wandered off into the future, and she saw her children running and playing on the balds, high on the Roan. *We will have a good life here, God willing.*

Above Isabelle, just below the roughly hewn mantel, was a stone with the mortar loose around it. Behind that river stone, where it had been placed all those years ago, was the gun. It was the gun her mother had used to protect herself from the soldier, and the gun that her father had hidden away. It was the very same gun that had caused her mother's shame and torment for the rest of her life. The truth, hidden all these years, was tucked behind the smooth stone, just a few inches from Isabelle's reach.

14

How, then, can they call on the one they have not believed in? And how can they believe in the one of whom they have not heard? And how can they hear without someone preaching to them?

~Romans 10:14

Welzia had traveled many hard miles in his life as a circuit preacher. Of course, many of those miles were the very same ones, traveled over and over again. Isabelle did not mind being a preacher's wife. She actually loved it. She knew that God had sent His calling to Welzia, and she knew you had to accept God's will. Welzia's brother, John Henry, preached as well. Like their father before them and their father's father before him. They were a preaching family. John Henry was Free Will Baptist, but Welzia was Methodist. There was some debate about this among the family, at first, but they decided that it was a choice each son had to make. Welzia held fast to his faith and soon became a cherished minister of the Roan Mountain area.

With several churches to attend to on his circuit, several weeks sometimes elapsed between visits from the preacher. When that happened, churches had regular services without one. Weddings were scheduled accordingly, as were baptisms.

On one cold morning, a few days before Welzia was scheduled to preach at a tiny church on the North Carolina side of the Roan, he was slowly moving through the deep woods, well on his way to his destination. It was a small white church, set back deep in the thick woodlands. The faithful members of the church came through the ice and snow or any bad weather, just to hear Welzia's sermon. He quickly became well known for his style of preaching, and he was held in high regard. The weather had turned decidedly worse, but Welzia did not turn back toward home.

Unwavering in his conviction, Welzia thought, *These good folks are looking forward to a preachin' and a preachin' they will have.*

The horse plodded along the creek heading into deeper and deeper snow. Welzia began to get more and more uneasy. He knew that his feet were now nearly frozen to the stirrups, but stopping here would not help the situation.

Up ahead, he caught sight of smoke curling up above the tree line. Coming in closer, he thought for sure that he could make out a cabin, set back a ways from the creek.

Sure enough, as he came closer, he could just make out the lamplight in the window. *Praise the Lord, my Rock and my Redeemer*, thought a grateful Welzia. *Here, yet again, God has provided me a warm sanctuary, just in time, and straight ahead.*

The path up to the cabin was treacherous. Each step the horse made slipped in the muck beneath the wet snow and caused Welzia growing concern. Dangerous trails like this could cause a horse to fall and break a leg. When weather like this was about, losing your horse could mean certain death.

Welzia carefully dismounted and guided his weary horse up the steep path. Once safe at the top, Welzia held the reins fast in his hand while he shouted out toward the cabin.

"Hello! Might there be anyone about?" The answer came in the creaking of the front door as it opened.

A face appeared in the dim light, and Welzia gave his name. The door had opened just slightly at first, but it suddenly slung open wide at the sound of "Arrowood," and a burly fellow with a full beard appeared in the doorway, filling it completely. Then the man shouted out, "Great Hosanna! It's the preacher man!"

The burly smiling man was Orbie McKinsey, a member of the little white church close by, who was obviously delighted to see the Minister.

Orbie clapped Welzia on the back and motioned him toward the fire and said, "Thaw ya'self on out, Preacher Man."

Welzia was heartily appreciative, and as he warmed himself by the fire, he talked about the service he would soon be holding at the little chapel and he recounted the snowy trip over the mountain as well.

Orbie's wife was just as portly as he was, and together, they made quite a couple.

Sudie McKinsey's cheeks had a glow of bright pink as she scurried about in the tiny kitchen. She was obviously in a hurry to serve up a warm meal, eager to help warm up the frozen minister. *Why, it's my womanly duty to help save the kind preacher from taking a chill*, she thought to herself as her breath came in puffs from her exertions. She had not a tooth left in her head, but that did not stop her from flashing a broad smile at the minister. She was pleased as punch to have him in her home, and she kept repeating this over and over to herself, smiling as she puttered.

Orbie quietly asked Sudie to hurry up and set the table, because "surely, the preacher was near to starving!" Welzia chuckled to himself at the spectacle the two were making. They were creating quite a noisy fuss over a small plate of beans and a biscuit, but to this couple it was as if they were serving him a platter-sized beefsteak. They were poor, humble servants of the Lord and Welzia appreciated their kindness and sacrifice of having to feed yet another hungry mouth.

Then, down from the rafters of the tiny cabin, there descended a whole passel of stair-step children. One after another they filed past, down from the loft bedroom where they had been sitting, quietly listening. Welzia stopped counting heads after a dozen or so had passed reverently by his chair, nodding and smiling.

Amazing, Welzia thought. *Simply amazing, that there are this many souls living in one small cabin.* No squalling or fussing was heard from the children as they had sat up in the loft, waiting to be called down. Calm and quiet reigned in this house. *It's simply amazing.* Welzia smiled in spite of himself and marveled at the thought of all those young'uns up there a-sleeping, stacked up like cord wood.

Orbie said, "Preacher Arrowood, take yourself a seat, now, and grab up a plate. Hope you brought a good appetite along with you." Welzia hung his hat on a peg by the fireplace and stood behind a chair at the table. The first round of eating was about to begin.

The meal was usually taken in shifts because there was only so much seating to be had around the small table. Sudie was a jovial soul as she puttered merrily around preparing the food. Her plump cheeks glowed even more brightly as the food filled the table. The cabin was bathed in the firelight. It was warm and snug, despite being quite crowded. All heads bowed, and all hands clasped together as a prayer was said over the food.

The Reverend Welzia spoke softly; his words flowed like molasses in his deep mountain drawl. He stood at the tableside with his head bowed to his chest, and his eyes closed and said, "We thank Thee, Lord, for providing us with the bounty spread before us. Let this food nourish our bodies and allow us to do Thy good works and glorify our Father, in heaven. Bless the hands that prepared the meal this day. Walk before us and prepare the way, Lord. Thy will be done. Amen!"

As the "Amen" still resonated in the air of the small cabin, there was a sudden commotion as the older kids moved toward the table and scurried to their spots. Welzia was served first, and all eyes were fixed intently upon him. No one would touch a bite until the honored guest had taken his first taste. All eyes were practically riveted on Welzia. As soon as he took a bite and nodded, then smiled in satisfaction, the happy chatter quickly resumed, filling the room.

The freckle-faced little girl with braided pigtails was somehow passed over when the plate of biscuits went around the table. A lively ruckus ensued before the father quickly intervened. After everyone had a biscuit, and all were satisfied, the children settled back down. The scowls on the puckered faces of the two little ones involved in the fray soon dissolved into smiles and the meal continued, uneventfully.

After seeing the smiles return, the tiny brows slowly becoming unruffled, and feeling confident that order was reestablished, Welzia felt a sudden twinge of sadness that he was not with his own brood. He longed to break bread at the head of his own family's table. He loved to take in the family's happy chatter and sharing, especially at mealtimes. It was his favorite time of the day, sitting quietly watching life unfold over the supper table. It was one of God's richest gifts. He smiled to himself and sent up a silent prayer that God would watch over his children and wife while he was absent from them.

This man is blessed, indeed. Blessed ever so much more than with just worldly riches, Welzia thought as he watched the laughter and smiles exchanged in the tiny, loving home. *There's more to life than gold in your pocket, so much more*, Welzia smiled as he thought.

After the meal was enjoyed, and everyone had eaten their fill, Welzia was offered a bedroll for the night and a designated place of honor near the fire, and he readily accepted the offer. After sleeping well, he got up early while it was still quite dark. Welzia well intended to ride toward the hills at first daylight, eager to get to the church and prepare his sermon. The flock was counting on him.

The family stood outside in the cold morning air to say their good-byes to Welzia. Sudie wrapped up two cold "cat head" biscuits and a large slab of cured ham in a small bundle and Welzia gratefully took it. When Sudie mentioned that they were "cat head" biscuits, he smiled, remembering his own mother calling them that, because they were so large, about the size of a cat's head.

Back at home, Isabelle had quickly settled back into life on the Roan. Here, she finally felt at peace. She knew this was where she was supposed to be. Sometimes, you just know these things without knowing why. And somehow, the 'whys', just didn't seem to matter so much.

She continued life, much in the same way her family always had on the Roan, but there were a few added conveniences. Welzia had built her a smokehouse for her meats and added a place to keep her butter from melting and the milk cold. He had dug out a depression in the creek bed where a bucket could be placed, and the cold mountain stream could flow around the bucket, keeping its contents cool. It was a mountain "refrigerator" long before the word was ever heard. He made a wooden lid that fit into the bucket securely, which helped insulate as well.

Life was hard here, as it had always been, but Isabelle had never even known what an easy life was. She knew that she had it so much better than her poor mother ever did. She beat their clothes on rocks in the stream to wash them and used the bark of the trees to die their homespun material. Out of this, she sewed their simple clothes. The mountain provided, just as it always had.

She remembered the herbs and medicinal plants her mother had taught her to use. She was a mother, wife, and nurse to many, there on the mountain, and nothing suited her better. She loved Welzia as much as he did her. Life was good on the Roan.

She was cleaning the cabin one day when she noticed the loose stone above the fireplace. It stirred up a distant memory in her instantly. She easily pulled it out and discovered the hidden gun. "I can't believe it's still here."

Once again, after all these years, sunlight gleamed off its metal. She knew who had hidden it there. All those years had passed by, and it had remained in place. She did not want to touch it. There were way too many bad memories surrounding that cold metal. She shuddered at the thought. Not wanting to touch it, she took the fire poker and picked up the gun through the finger hole on the trigger.

Carefully, she took the gun over to the bed and wrapped it in an old piece of cloth and tied it up tight with string. Welzia would know what to do with it, she quickly surmised. Welzia would take care of it, and she would never have to see it again. Leaving that gun in the house was just not something she could ever allow. It just had to be removed. Gone entirely would be even better.

The years passed. Welzia had hidden the gun out in the smokehouse, away from Isabelle, and she soon forgot about it. Or so he hoped. He was very protective of her and did not want her upset anymore over the gun. She had hurt enough in her life.

They had the rest of their children, and the little family grew, year by year. Life was good to the family. The cabin seemed to become smaller and smaller, and more cramped with each addition to the family. Welzia was very good at woodworking—actually he was quite handy at most things. So they soon decided to build onto the cabin, and they did just that, in stages, over the years. It was just after the eldest girl started her schooling that he decided to add the second floor.

When the walls were being replaced, and new studs were added, he brought the gun, still wrapped up in the bundle, inside the house when Isabelle was out working her garden patch. He did not want her to see. He carefully removed the gun from the old cloth and placed it in the wall. He closed it in, nailing it away forever, or so he thought. She would never have to look at it and feel pain again. And the gun was where it would never cause pain and death ever again. He felt great satisfaction with the pounding of each nail as the wall sealed the gun away.

The years came swiftly on the Roan, and Welzia and Isabelle grew old together. The years floated past, like fallen leaves floating on the surface of a fast-moving, clear mountain stream. God continued to watch over this family. Their children, now grown, soon began having children of their own.

Isabelle sat in her rocking chair as her little granddaughter softly called out to her on the porch. "It's time, Grandma," Star Rella said. "It's time for supper. Hal brought in some vegetables fresh from the garden."

These grandchildren were children of her youngest son, Fred.

Isabelle rose from her chair and winced from the sharp pain in her wrist as she balanced herself with one hand. *Getting way too old*, she thought to herself. "I'm older than thunder," she chuckled. "Older than thunder, and then some." But Isabelle's eyes were still clear, expressive, and incredibly blue. Held deep in her eyes was the reflection of her younger self, still the beautiful eyes of the girl she once was.

Isabelle's blue eyes misted over as she traveled back in her mind, to earlier days. She heard the bubbling laughter as her son, Lewis William, nicknamed 'Pat', a twin to her Esther, made another one of his flawless imitations of a bird's call. He was a blond-haired, blue-eyed boy, eagerly inquisitive and full of life, always with a ready smile and a happy heart. He practiced his bird calls each evening, and he listened intently while out in the woods, learning each call. He was always gathering up the world around him, absorbing each moment. Each bird's song he mimicked was distinct and beautiful in the waning sunlight. Pat reminded Isabelle of his baby brother Samuel, who choked to death on a peach pit while just a toddler. Isabelle grieved still, over the devastating loss of little Samuel. Pat was always such a thoughtful child, certainly a favored child of Isabelle's, among her twelve beloved children. Now, Pat was grown, with a family of his own, living down in the Piedmont of the Carolinas, working in the cotton mills there. Pat had married a beautiful dark-haired girl named Edith, who had sadly died soon after giving birth to a blond-haired son named Ray Everett. Pat had remarried not long after losing Edith, to another dark-haired beauty named Maude. She was a Hull. This family came from over in Lincoln County, North Carolina, where many had moved from to seek work in the Carolina mill boom.

The family had always gathered on the porch when the evenings arrived on the mountain. As the fading sunlight turned the puffy white clouds to a golden pink hue, all eyes would watch the horizon. Night closed in on the Roan gradually, with the lessening light. It was a cherished time of day when the family came together, the hard day's work complete.

In the evenings, the air cooled, and the mist slowly settled in, like a blanket on the mountain made of pure spun wool. Music was made, with banjos twanging out a familiar tune and fiddles singing out merrily, and all the family's voices chiming in with gusto. The voices blended like only sibling's voices can. Of course, Pat's bird imitations were the night's crowning moment. The whole family looked forward to these gatherings with anticipation.

You were just about certain that it was an actual bird making the sounds when Pat had gotten good and wound up in the moment. These were the days before radio or television had made its way to the mountain, and the only entertainment available was the entertainment they made for themselves.

Isabelle missed those simpler times, especially now, and these days the evenings were getting a bit too cold for her old bones to sit out on the porch, come evening time. Most of the older children were all grown and gone, seeking to live their lives.

Her beloved Welzia was gone now, too, ten years in the ground. The love of her life, her rock, and now in the twilight of her years, she was left here without him. It just did not seem right to her. But she knew God was in his heaven and that He knew best.

The Roan looked on, watching the generations pass, her trees growing taller, with the endless music wafting over the pines in the pale moonlight. *She will remain for many generations to come,* Isabelle thought. *Oh, this beautiful old mountain that I love so well. She will outlast us all, no doubt about it.*

She knew it wouldn't be long now, and she would be with her Welzia again and with the good Lord. She was ready—she knew it was near her time. Whenever He decided it was time to call her, she knew it would be the right time. It was true what the old folks had always said: you do outlive your usefulness. *What a shame,* she thought. *I can't crochet anymore. Why, I can't hardly even hold the needle.* She had so wanted to make some booties for the newest little great-grandchild. She had even chosen the perfect yarn.

She absently rubbed her aching wrist and thought, *The weather is movin' in fast over the mountain, I can feel it down deep in my bones.* She reached into the deep pocket of her apron, and her seeking fingertips found what she was searching for.

The buckeye. She carried it with her, always. The buckeye was given to her as a child by her father. It was believed to help ward off the pain of arthritis, when carried in your pocket and was considered somewhat magical by the Indians as well. Not totally sure it worked at all, she carried it anyway. It was what the people of the mountain did, so it seemed perfectly natural to Isabelle. She smiled at the touch of it. It was a token of love more precious to her than gold.

Her mother, Nancy, would have been so proud to see her family. She would have been so very proud to see all these beautiful children who had been born of her line. She would be "tickled pink," as Nancy loved to say, to know that she had a beautiful little Chloe in the family. Isabelle smiled at the thought, *Pretty little dark-haired Chloe, just the spitting image of her great-grandmother.*

There was yet another beautiful great-granddaughter, named after little Mary Calla. *God rest her soul, my precious sister. She missed out on so much in life. It's brought me much sadness through all these years, being without her, but I know she has kept watch over me. I have felt her close by me while watching a butterfly flit past. Always, it was a fleeting moment of joy with one of God's perfect creations, but also there was a feeling, a deep knowing, that it was Calla's spirit fluttering past. I have felt her in the sweet winds that blow off the Roan. She is here in this beautiful place; I just know she is.* Isabelle smiled, and from her clear blue eyes, tears formed and fell, rolling down her weathered cheeks.

Isabelle had lived a good life and taught her children to love the Lord. She was forever trying to sow fertile seeds in her children, planting the very seeds that would help them find their way through life. The same seeds her dear mother had sown. She remembered something that her mother had always told her: "Measure your days here on Earth not by what you may reap, but by the seeds you have sown." Isabelle had sown her seeds well. She constantly prayed that her mother and father had finally found the peace that had been taken from them. She prayed they were together in heaven. She prayed for her family and their children that were just beginning to make their way in life. She felt content that God would watch over these children of the Roan.

Peace finally came to Isabelle, later in the fall of the year, and they laid her to rest beside her beloved Welzia, beneath the old stand of short weathered pines that overlooked the balds, high on the Roan. It was her favorite spot.

No prettier place could be found on the mountain in springtime when the grasses turn an amazing green, and fields of endless wildflowers sway in the light breeze. The mountain laurel blooms profusely, and for as far as you could see, there is a vast wave of rolling fuchsia. The mountain ridges are virtually painted with the pinkish-purple color. These ridges are surely painted with a heavenly brush, the brush that is held in the mighty hand of God. Just one look over that rolling ridge and you are swallowed up in God's overwhelming presence.

Isabelle rests now, beneath the green grass as the sweet mountain breezes blow over her. Whispers in the pines call out her name from time to time, and the whip-poor-will replies.

The Roan never forgets.

The house was handed down through two more generations after Isabelle's passing. Like the Roan, the house saw its children come and go. The years brought their share of laughter, as well as occasional tears. Many coats of paint were added to the old house. The rooms were redone, one by one. The porch was added, the front room was enlarged, but the hall never really changed. It was the center of the house, the heart of the house. The original wood had such a beautiful glow that no one could bring themselves to change it. A good polishing was all it ever needed.

Hidden deep inside the wall, just down the hall in the center of the house the gun remained. Its secret hidden in the darkness, safe, for many years, until Jane's homecoming brought it back into the bright light of day.

15

The golden moments in the stream of life rush past us and we see nothing but sand; the angels come to visit us, and we only know them when they are gone.

~George Elliot

Jane gathered up two more big bundles of the tattered and yellowed letters, and she carried them into the living room and laid them on the couch beside her.

She had been reading for hours, but she just couldn't stop, not now. She could hardly wait to open the next bundle, but she needed a cup of coffee to hold and warm her hands. She hurriedly fixed one and practically ran back to the couch. Careful not to spill the coffee, she placed it down on the end table and then plopped herself down and settled into the cushions, comfortably.

While reaching out and turning on the lamp, to light the darkening room, it suddenly occurred to her: "The gun, could it possibly be the same one that I found? Oh, my goodness, it has to be," she whispered as the realization dawned on her, with her hand still resting on the switch. Her heart skipped a beat, and she wasted not a second more to untie another ribbon.

Doll Flats

Sarah Ellen was a very intelligent girl. She knew that her family was a bit different from most of the locals who lived in the area. It didn't bother her too much—she accepted it with much more savvy than her tender years allowed. She would be turning thirteen on her birthday, and her sharp wit had gotten her out of many situations that most thirteen-year-olds would never have found themselves in, in the first place.

She had a reputation for being the most levelheaded and mild-mannered of all her siblings. The whole lot was incorrigible but still lovable, or at least they were to Sarah Ellen. Most in the family called her Sarah "Ellender." It was the mountain way, she supposed, and who was she to question it?

Sarah Ellender's family had lived here on the mountain for many generations. She knew the paths through the woods better than most. She ran over the fields and along the winding path like the wind. She ran with her long blond hair trailing out wildly behind her. Springtime on the mountain was especially nice this year. It was an unusually warm one. There was no late frost that usually killed the blossoms as they first emerged their tiny, frail heads.

The smell of the mountain laurel and all the wildflowers in full bloom would be the only smell that could compare to the one blowing off the mountain right now. Of course, it was way too early for the mountain laurel. Just getting outside after a long, cold winter was such joy that Sarah Ellender could hardly stand it. So instead of walking as a young lady should, she ran.

Besides, her birthday was coming in May, and who said you couldn't be happy near the time of your very own birthday?

As she ran, she thought about her brother John. She loved John very much. They were close in age, and they had an unspoken understanding between them, one that did not exist between her and the rest of her siblings. *It's just as simple as that*, she thought with a light laugh. John was her favorite, and the rest were simply, well, her brothers and sisters. Words weren't even necessary between them, right from the beginning. *But I guess I do love John a tad more than all the rest, even if Momma tells me that it isn't right,* Sarah Ellender thought with a slight pout. *It's not right to tell a person how they are supposed to feel in their own heart. Now that's what's not right.*

She had felt an even closer bond to John after their sister Mary Nancy had died five years back. Mary Nancy was only nine years old, with Sarah just a year younger, when the fever came and took her. Sarah Ellender didn't understand why the fever killed Mary Nancy and not all of them. They all had the fever, of course; the whole family did, but for some reason, poor Mary Nancy got it worst of all.

Maybe God took Mary Nancy because God needed a sweet-faced angel in heaven. He sure didn't take me. I must not be good, and I'm sure that I'm not even a bit sweet-faced, she thought with a grimace. *Well, I'm sure glad that the fever didn't take me on up to the angels, because if the fever had taken me, too, I wouldn't be getting to smell my birthday a-coming right now.* Sarah Ellender had associated the smell of green spring grass and wildflowers as a precursor to her birthday from a very young age.

She ran a bit faster and said a quick prayer that God would take good care of Mary Nancy and that she sure hoped she was happy up in heaven. She hoped that angels were there with her, keeping her company, and lots of them. She shuddered when she thought of the day that Mary Nancy passed. She was very sick herself, but she remembered how terrible it was.

Momma was crying and wringing her hands. Then she wailed. She just up and threw back her head and wailed. Sarah Ellender was scared. She was in the bed, lying beside Mary Nancy when the fever took her. Sarah Ellender lay back on the bed, terribly weak and frightened that the fever was coming to take her, too.

Momma had never wailed or made a sound anywhere near to what she did that day. Sometimes, when Sarah Ellender was drifting off to sleep, she heard her momma's wail. It would startle her so bad that the whole bed would shake.

She would never be able to forget that tormented sound, not ever.

They waited until the ground had thawed out some to bury her sister. She remembered when the wagon was loaded up with the small casket. The horse was hitched to the wagon right out in front of the house. The two Guinn boys, from down across the hollow, came and put the small wooden box onto the wagon. They were twins. They were big boys and really strong.

Then they all walked behind the wagon, over the hill to Shell Creek. It was the first funeral procession that Sarah Ellender had ever attended.

The walk to the cemetery had been slow, and the wind had blown something fierce, Sarah Ellen remembered well. Coughing was heard clear across the way, as most of those attending the funeral were sick themselves. *When the bad sickness came, it seemed to come to each and every house on the mountain*, Sarah thought.

The fever took two more children in the same hollow and another, two hollows away. Sarah wondered what it was like to die. Her momma had always told her that the "Good Lord will watch over you" and that he was watching over Mary Nancy every day. Sarah Ellender thought, *Even God must get tired of watching over everybody. Maybe the angels helped Him some, with all that watching to do.* It sure made sense to her.

She missed sweet Mary Nancy. She had always let Sarah Ellender play with her corn-husk dolly, and even let her play with her special rocks, the ones that she loved so. Mary Nancy had always looked for pretty-colored stones in the creek. She loved them dearly.

Sarah Ellender had found such stones herself when playing in Shell Creek. She carefully placed the prettiest stones that she could find on the ground where Mary Nancy was buried. *That way she can look down from Heaven and see them, and know that I love her and miss her.*

Sarah ran even faster, and the wind made a whooshing noise as it blew past her ears. She held out her arms and pretended she was flying, flying high like the birds that soar up and over the Roan.

The land on the Roan was settled by her grandpa Shell's family. His father and his father before him had come to live on this land years ago. Most all the Shells in the area were kin to her.

Momma was a Shell a'fore she married father. Then, when she married, she became a Winters. Strange how when you marry up, you aren't who you used to be anymore, mused Sarah Ellender as she wrinkled the tip of her nose.

Time passed on by when no one was looking. Sarah Ellender had just turned sixteen, but she still ran, even though everyone thought it was not very ladylike. She had run nonstop this day until she was back on the ridge overlooking her home. She had just come from the next hollow over, to visit with Mrs. Carraway. She had heard she had taken real bad sick while attending church services, and she wanted to check in on her.

Sarah Ellender knew by heart, each medicinal plant that grew wild on the Roan and what sickness could be cured with it. She knew most everything had a use and a purpose. God didn't waste anything at all. She had been taught all of this by her sweet grandmother Shell that lived over on Shell Creek. Why, Grandma Polly knew that mountain like the back of her hand. Just about every malady that a body could get, she felt confident that the mountain could cure it. People just knew to go to Polly when they needed curing. Didn't much matter what it was, either.

She had told Sarah Ellender that "knowing the right plant could mean the difference between a life saved and a life lost." Sarah Ellender had listened intently to the years of Granny Polly's instruction, and she had learned well. She had practically indexed the whole mountain in her sharp mind. *When I gathered the bark from the holly tree to make a soothing tea for Alice Denton's little boy who had the colic, my goodness, was Grandma Polly ever so proud!* thought Sarah Ellender as she smiled. There wasn't a doctor for miles, but the folks on the Roan did not worry too much about it. They had Granny Polly, and now they had Sarah Ellender, as well.

She turned and left the ridge, and as she ran back toward home, she heard a booming voice echoing across the meadow. There seemed to be some commotion just out of sight, on the path ahead behind the trees. She sprinted on and skidded to a sudden stop when she saw from where the noise was coming. It was her father, Billy Winters, shouting out orders to two cousins. His sled had gotten stuck on a stump, and he did not "cotton" to the idea of being stuck and unable to move. You could tell he was more than just a bit irate.

Billy was nearly crippled, and walking had long since become very painful for him. All the years of fighting, hard work, and, of course, his infamous shenanigans had finally taken their toll on his bones.

So, to be able to continue his role of being "the boss of the Winters clan," he had his sons fashion him a sled of sorts. A fine feather bed was attached to the sleigh, and he directed the boys to pull him around on the sled so that he could oversee what needed to be attended to around the farm. What a sight he made, lying up there on that bed, being pulled all around. All the while, his cane was held high aloft as he barked out his directions to those who were doing the pulling. Billy had become quite a grouch because of his difficulty in walking, but Sarah Ellender saw through his gruff nature, choosing to see straight through the bad to the tender side he kept well hidden. She sometimes imagined that the soft side of her father lay just below the hard surface. She had not a clue that this tender side was reserved for her and her alone. Sarah was quite alone in her opinion of her father. In fact, most in the area simply referred to him as "mean old man Winters."

"What's all this fuss about, Father?" Sarah Ellender said as she came closer. "Why, I could hear the ruckus you were making from clear across the meadow."

Love and Mercy - Up On Roan Mountain

The scowl melted away, and a sudden smile played across Billy's face at the sight of his beloved Sarah Ellender. Even his deeply furrowed brow smoothed right out. *Amazing how he can change his whole looks in just one second*, she thought. *He's really just an old softy.*

"I want to get this sled over this dad-blasted stump and back on up to the house, so I can have my supper today, not tomorrow," Billy roared out in his usual manner.

But his anger diminished as he again looked lovingly at Sarah Ellender and thought, with a smile, *Amazing how a freckle-faced child can transform into a beautiful young woman, just about overnight.*

The four boys who were attending to the task of pulling Billy shrunk visibly at the sheer volume of his voice. Sarah Ellender stayed with her father for a few moments more, talking to him soothingly, trying to calm him so that the boys had time to tug the heavy sled over the stump. They moved him back onto the trail and were soon off again. Then another loud bellow rang out from Billy, and Sarah looked back. The sled had suddenly lurched over a rock on the path, nearly launching Billy from his bed. Sarah Ellender could not keep herself from laughing, which she stifled quickly by clamping her hand over her mouth. At her last glimpse, her father still had his cane raised high in the air angrily.

When they were safely on their way back to the house, Sarah Ellender sighed. She turned and looked out over the mountain. Along with most who lived on it, she dearly loved this old mountain and thought of the Roan as her very own.

The day's light was beginning to fade, and the sun began to sink lower in the sky, and everything took on a pink, almost peachy glow. Sarah Ellender adored this time of day.

The Roan watches over us all, she thought. She turned after one last look and then, reluctantly, she headed back up toward the house, to see about helping her mother get supper ready. She had purposely allowed herself a generous amount of time before heading that way. She did not want to have to listen to the constant complaints that her father was surely doling out to those poor boys with each errant bump. Sarah Ellender giggled at the thought. *Oh, Father, what a bad egg you are.*

The years passed swiftly, and Sarah Ellender had reached proper courting age. She had blossomed into quite a handsome woman. Strong willed and bold in nature, but with soft eyes and incredibly long lashes. Her piercing blue eyes seemed to change color subtly from a clear blue to a hazy gray, depending on her mood. Possession of all these attributes was quite a formidable combination in a young girl. The men in her family were very protective of her, and with a family like hers, her suitors could not be timid of heart. The timid had not even a snowball's chance of survival among her ornery and protective brothers.

Sarah giggled at the thought of what it must be like for a fellow to come court the sister of one of the "Devils." *Quite scary for sure, enough to have the boy shaking in his boots*, she thought with a chuckle.

Sarah's mother, Eliza, had been told by most that marrying Billy Winters was not the best choice she could make. "Think twice and then think again, I tell you," said the older ladies in church one day, to a young Eliza.

But, of course, love wants what love wants.

She loved him, and there was no changing that. Eliza married the wild, untamed Billy Winters, and they settled down, built a home on the Doll Flats, and started a family of their own. Or rather, Eliza settled down, kept the house, and Billy continued being, well, Billy.

The townsfolk whispered among themselves about it. Billy was somewhat of a wanderer and a wild soul. He would challenge just about anybody to a fighting match. "That devil Billy must have some more devils a-chasing after him," the people said in lowered voices. The couple truly loved each other; that was certain. But still Billy would leave Eliza and run all over the county when his wanderlust proved to be too much. He would be gone for months and leave poor

Eliza to care for her brood alone. But Billy did provide for his family—he made sure she had food to feed them, and plenty of it.

They had more children than you could shake a stick at during their marriage. There were three children lost in childbirth, and seven boys and seven girls lived. These children grew up quickly, in the area of the Roan called the Doll Flats. Every summer Billy would hold "tough man" contests and people would come in wagons from all around to watch the fights.

When their boys were old enough, they fought in the fights as well. This caused Eliza to be hopping mad, but there was little to be done about it.

Sarah Ellender did not enjoy the fights in the least, and she made sure she stayed away when the brawling commenced. They got rough, and the boys would fistfight until the last man was standing, and a winner was declared. Watching such a spectacle was downright immoral in Sarah Ellender's eyes.

What possessed her brothers to partake in such foolishness was beyond Sarah Ellender's comprehension. *Sometimes,* she thought, *grown men can act just like silly little boys.* She knew that one day it would not end well for someone. The excitement that these games drew was all the more bewildering to Sarah Ellender. But whatever caused the people to come by the dozens and watch definitely had some kind of effect over them. They came in by wagon loads. Wagon after wagon came up the winding road to the house and camped out in the grassy fields on the Doll Flats. At every event, Sarah Ellender marveled at the idiocy of it. She thought, *Such nonsense, and not one in the crowd that wasn't bleeding somewhere, by the end of it all.* "Men," she said under her breath. As she grew older and wiser, the urgent need to get away from the violent fighting was growing, as well.

Sam Arrowood was, in fact, her very own knight who had ridden over the mountain to save her, but Sarah Ellender didn't know any such thing. She knew very little about Sam and possessed even less inclination to know more. But, without a doubt, he was the one for Sarah Ellender.

She went to the church services each Sunday, as she usually did, but this time the visiting circuit minister, Samuel Augustus Arrowood, met her at the door. He was tall, blond-haired, and most handsome. His shoulders were wide and strong, filling out the suit he wore, which was still a bit dusty from his ride in. She extended her hand, cordially, and introduced herself. Sam took Sarah Ellender's hand in his with a smile. Afterward, during the service, Sam could hardly keep his mind on the sermon he had planned to deliver that day. Sarah Ellender somehow knew that Sam was different from the rest, but she was still very skeptical of all men.

There were other ministers in Sam's family as well. That fact somehow made Sarah Ellender think more highly of him. Just knowing that his family was upstanding and decent made a big difference with her.

Sam was a quiet, gentle man with soul-searching eyes. He carried his beloved Bible in his hand wherever he went. Sam got the calling to preach in his early teens, and he knew what the Lord expected of him. Early on, Sam would walk high on the ridge overlooking Rock Creek, where some of his family farmed, to practice his preaching. The wind and the trees were his congregation at first, and he delivered up stirring messages of hope and repentance. His voice quickly transformed and lost its quiet and meek sound, and became emboldened and strong when he preached. He was perfect for it. Born to it, most would say.

The pews were filled wherever he went to preach. His sermons were all delivered with a soulful determination and sincerity that left the people listening entranced. He saved many lost souls for the Lord, and he knew in his heart that he was doing what God himself had designed him to do.

Sarah Ellender was not a likely choice of wife for a minister. But Sam saw through the Winters clan's reputation and saw Sarah Ellender for who she was.

Love and Mercy - Up On Roan Mountain

She was a kind, and tenderhearted girl who wanted a better life and someone she could trust to share her life. She was intelligent, and she also knew her own mind and didn't let others sway her way of thinking. Sam saw her qualities instantly and knew she was the one.

After the church service was over, tables were set up on the grassy field right behind the church, overlooking the meadows. Starched cotton tablecloths billowed out in the warm breeze that day, startlingly white in the bright sunshine. The unmistakable smell of fried chicken, biscuits, and seasoned green beans, that wonderful "dinner on the grounds" smell, filled the air. Bees buzzed and flitted from one flower to the next, and the white blossoms of the apple trees nearby tumbled in the wind like a springtime snowfall. Spring, the perfect time for a budding romance.

Sam found himself crowded smack-dab in the middle of four ample-bodied church women who had suddenly cornered him for information. They wanted to know about the health of his mother, Fannia. His mother had gone to Blount County, a week or so back, to be with Sam's sister Fannie. Fannie had married a Whitehead, and she was nearing time to deliver her first baby and she needed her mother there with her.

Sam half stumbled backwards a step, when the women crowded closer around him, with his back to the church steps. Sally Mitchum asked, "So, Sam, when do you think the baby's due to come?"

But, before Sam even had a chance to answer, Mrs. Hobson imploringly asked, "How'd your dear mother fare after that wagon ride over the mountain? That had to be pretty hard on her bones, jostling over that mountain, what with her rheumatism more than likely acting up." With more questions shot at him in rapid fire succession, and then even more excited chattering erupting among the women, Sam became totally bumfuzzled and didn't know which question to answer first. He really couldn't concentrate on talking to these women, for he had eyes for Sarah Ellender only, that day.

As he stood towering above the heads of the chattering group of women, Sam's view was unobstructed. He stood there, smiling broadly, thinking that his view was ever so nice. Sarah Ellender was placing the bowls of food onto the table and tying down the corners of the tablecloths to prevent the wind from catching them and blowing them off. Her graceful movements and the way she held her head aloft, so self-assured and with determination, held Sam's attention captive.

She doesn't even know how beautiful she really is, standing there in the sunlight, with the wind blowing her dress and her hair out behind her. The apple blossoms are billowing around her like a shower of snow. She hasn't even a clue, Sam thought. His heart was smitten.

Sarah Ellender, on the other hand, wasn't at all that interested in Samuel. She looked up and saw him staring and stupidly smiling straight at her. She instantly lowered her eyes and turned away, scowling. She could plainly see that Sam was handsome, but they all were if you wanted them to be. They all chased after the pretty girls, never mind if those girls had a brain at all. Smart girls didn't matter to boys, not one bit.

Sarah Ellender had been around enough brash loudmouthed men to have grown quite savvy in her short years. She was looking for more than looks because looks fade over time. The truth is; looks don't amount to a hill of beans, as far as she was concerned.

She wanted someone she could believe in, someone she could trust. She wanted someone who would be there for her, always. She was looking for the kind of support in a life mate that her dear mother never really had. Sarah Ellender was not going to have her mother's life of uncertainty. She was not going to be left at home with a whole houseful of hungry kids tugging on her, and another on the way, and no husband in sight. Not her. Not ever.

From the steady stream of young boys who made their way to the Doll Flats enticed with the fights, Sarah Ellender had seen enough of men to leave her jaded. She had punched more than just a few noses and wasn't afraid to defend herself again, should the occasion arise. She was going to find herself the right man, or she would never get married at all. That attitude suited her fine and dandy.

Her mother, Eliza, saw the matter entirely differently. She had told her many times, "Don't be so quick to run off every suitor, Sarah girl. Before too long, you will be considered an old maid."

"Oh, Mother. An old maid at seventeen?" Sarah Ellender laughed. "I know you love me, and you want what's best for me. But there is no law that says you have to marry up, not ever." She had her standards, and she was not a girl who would ever settle for less.

Sam was soft-spoken and considered somewhat meek by many who knew him, and surely he did not have a clue as to what he was up against with Sarah Ellender. As to whether or not he could win her over, that remained to be seen.

But love always wants what love wants.

16

"For I know the plans I have for you, declares the Lord, plans to prosper you and not to harm you, plans to give you hope and a future."

~ Jeremiah 29:11

Change was surely in the wind, but up on the Roan, most changes were barely felt. Tennessee was at the forefront of political change, but for those living way back up in the hills of Tennessee life continued much the same way that it always had.

Samuel had, after a dozen or more tries, finally succeeded getting Sarah Ellender to consent to go on a picnic with him, out on the field just beyond her home on the Doll Flats. The picnic was well within sight of the porch where her father, Billy, sat with his cane in his hand. Out in the open field was the only place suitable for a picnic, Billy himself had decided this resolutely. Sarah Ellender had reluctantly agreed, after her mother's insistent prodding. Boys were the last thing on Sarah Ellender's mind. She was worried about her Granny Polly. She had been ill for more than a solid week now, and none of the regular remedies seemed to be working for her.

Samuel tried his best to gain Sarah Ellender's attention and affection, but he failed miserably with each new attempt. But somehow, he kept faith in his heart that she would begin to love him and that she would marry him, eventually.

Privately, talk and rumors had slowly begun to circulate about a possible war to abolish slavery, but public discussion was prohibited at the time. But, for the most part, there were no slaves owned by the people on the mountain, as they were poor farmers. "But if there were slave owners living here, the people of the Roan wouldn't have ever allowed it to begin with," Sarah Ellender said with conviction. Then she bit into a piece of fried chicken that Sam had brought in the basket. "They just naturally know in their hearts that holding another person in bondage is just not right."

Eastern Tennessee had established a strong antislavery sentiment early on, during the years leading up to the Civil War. "Why Minnesota is now the thirty-second state of America," said Sarah Ellender with a curt nod of her head. "We are growing as a nation, by leaps and bounds." "We can't just continue with the senseless idea that owning a person as a slave is right." "They are surely God's children, too."

Samuel blinked slowly and tried to take it all in. *This slip of a girl, raised up on a mountain, knows more about what is going on in the world than I do*, Samuel thought in amazement. Her intelligence was a force to be reckoned with, and he was in total awe.

Samuel had worked hard on the farm and had gathered all the skills required of a farmer. He knew how to plant, and when to plant each crop, according to the signs, and when it was time to harvest. He knew his Bible and could quote scripture with the best of them. He certainly knew his way around the plow and that knowledge, along with his lifelong study of God's word, was about the full extent of his education. He was not dumb, by any means, but he had never really been exposed to someone like Sarah Ellender before. His family was well known for its ingenuity. They could make things work for them, no matter what they set about to do.

Sarah Ellender had opened up a totally new way of looking at things for Samuel. This new perspective was amazing to him. He had never met anyone quite like her. She was every bit as smart as she was beautiful.

But her brothers were always near, keeping a careful watch over their sister. They could be intimidating, to say the least. Her brother John was smarter than most, but he loved Sarah Ellender deeply, and he had warned Samuel that should he ever hurt one golden hair on her head, he would have to answer to him. Samuel never wanted any harm to come to his beloved Sarah Ellender, but sometimes brothers just can't see what's right before them.

John had been instructed by his father to watch over Samuel, and make sure that Sarah Ellender was safe. His father knew how much John loved his sister. John fully intended to watch over his sister, even before Billy had given him his instructions.

The farm was always swarming with people who came to watch and partake in the fighting. John enjoyed a good brawl as much as the next fellow, but when it came to Sarah Ellender, no one was going to get near her while he was nearby.

Many a young man had tried, and many had left bruised, battered, and sometimes bleeding because of it. But John finally came around to see that Samuel was different. He knew that Samuel came from a good family and that he had good, honest intentions toward Sarah Ellender. John wanted to see Sarah settled down and happy, and in his way of thinking, that meant safe from harm as well. After a heated discussion, John Henry and Samuel became good and fast friends. Their main bond was the strong love they each felt for Sarah Ellender.

Samuel's intense religious upbringing was perfectly balanced by the rougher upbringing of Sarah Ellender, and together they worked well. One complemented and somehow tempered the other.

The wedding bells soon rang out for this happy couple. Sarah Ellender finally saw Samuel for the kind, sweet man that he was, and Samuel finally accepted how downright stubborn, beautiful Sarah Ellender could be. But again, the one complemented the other, and together they were complete.

Even Billy finally came around and agreed to the union of the two. He did have his own "word of prayer" with a pale-faced Samuel behind the barn one afternoon before the wedding. But all distrust was eventually laid aside, and Billy gave his blessings.

One by one, Sarah Ellender's other brothers promised a wide-eyed Samuel that they would knock a knot on his head if he ever so much as misspoke to—let alone mistreated—their Sarah Ellender. Samuel was pretty sure that every last one of them meant it, too.

With a family such as the Winters clan, you didn't want to mess around and make any of them mad. Samuel did not intend to do any such thing.

On a bright spring day, Samuel and Sarah Ellender married in Yancey County, North Carolina. The bride was glowing and happy; with wildflowers circling her head and trailing off behind in her long hair. She wore her very best dress. She never looked more beautiful.

John stood by proudly as he witnessed the union. Sarah Ellender's younger sister, Mary Jane caught the bouquet as Sarah Ellender tossed it over her shoulder. Mary Jane was married herself less than a year later.

Sarah stood and looked at her younger siblings and remembered when each had come along. *One by one, they seemed to just get meaner and meaner*, she thought with a grin. *But I sure do love them, mean and all.*

Little Malinda, whom Sarah Ellender called "Lindie," was about five years younger than her. She watched Lindie now, smiling and acting all respectable. But she remembered her as just a small thing, with her hair a tangled mess and dirt-streaked cheeks, standing by the bridge over the creek with her brothers Daniel, Albert, and

Martin. She was every bit as mean as the boys were as she stood beside them demanding money from kids who crossed over the bridge on their way to school. If they had no money to pay for their passage, Sarah's siblings would take whatever they could from the kids. They were a band of junior extortionists in the making. Sarah Ellender shook her head as she remembered, laughing, "What bad eggs they all were."

Sarah Ellender laughed out loud in spite of herself as she remembered how her father took that news. When he found out what the children had been up to, he roared so loudly that it was heard at least three hollows over. Sarah Ellender held her hand to her mouth to hide her mirth. Now, being the first daughter to leave the nest, she felt like she was leaving the duty of watching over her younger siblings behind her. This thought caused a tear to slide down her cheek, in spite of how happy she was.

Her mother, Eliza, had just given birth to another baby boy, one month ago. Sarah Ellender figured after Mary Jane was married and gone, that it would fall upon little Lindie to step up and help her mother with her siblings. *Mean little tightfisted Lindie, watching over those poor unsuspecting children, they will hardly stand a chance*, Sarah Ellender thought with a cluck of her tongue and a shake of her head.

Sarah Ellender and Samuel built themselves a little cabin up along Big Rock Creek. Samuel was eager to get started planting his crops, but the dogwood trees were not yet in bloom. "I was always told that you plant your corn when the dogwood trees are in full bloom," Sarah Ellender said. "That is, usually after dogwood winter."

Samuel said, "What is this dogwood winter?"

Sarah Ellender laughed and said, "Well, now, if'n you had been raised up on the Roan, you would naturally just know. Right before the dogwood comes into bloom, we usually have a cold snap. After they bloom, it usually warms back up. Then you wait until blackberry winter."

Love and Mercy - Up On Roan Mountain

"Oh?" Samuel said, smiling. "What in the world is that?"

"Another cold snap that usually comes when the blackberry bushes are in bloom," said Sarah Ellender with a laugh. "My goodness, I thought you told me you were a farming man!"

Samuel picked up Sarah Ellender at the waist and spun her around before setting her back down lightly onto the floor. "You did marry a farming man, my pretty wife. And a preaching man, to boot!"

"But maybe you'd fare better being the one doing all the preaching." They laughed together, and Samuel kissed her lightly. She smiled up at him, and she knew she had chosen the only man for her.

Sarah Ellender was hanging her wash out to dry one morning, and she caught sight of a large red bird she had never seen before on the Roan. She followed it into the edge of the woods where it lit on an elm tree. She stood still and admired the pretty bird, and it suddenly crowed like a bantam rooster. Amazed, she watched until it flew off the branch, winging its way toward the valley.

As she made her way back to the house, she saw a patch of ramps growing by the creek, up just a way further. She made her way toward the patch through the brambles. *Ramps would be a great addition to our supper*, thought a pleased Sarah Ellender. Once down by the creek side, she saw an old turtle sitting on a large rock overlooking the creek. As she drew closer, she realized that the poor turtle was dead. As she peered over the rock, she saw below it, near the stream, another turtle that was looking up in the direction of the dead turtle.

She returned to the spot three days later to gather more ramps and some branch lettuce, and the turtle was still there. Apparently the dead turtle was being watched over by its mate. The turtle had stayed by its side, waiting. *What a pitiful thing to witness*, she thought, and it caused her sadness to think that the turtle would wait in vain. She saw this as an omen, and it frightened her. She hurried home and worried over the turtle, until her Samuel came home for supper, safe.

Her mother had come down the following day to search for some bead bush trees. The trees were called "bead bush" because of the seed pods that looked like beads that formed in the fall after the tree bloomed. Its forked limbs were sometimes used as divining rods. These divining rods were used to locate underground water.

In the past, Billy had used the divining rods whenever he wanted to locate and dig out a water well. After Eliza had located the bead bush trees and had gathered her limbs, she went to get a cool drink from the creek.

When she went down the bank, closer to the creek, she saw the same turtle that Sarah Ellender had seen, still waiting for its dead mate below the large rock.

Eliza saw it as the same omen that Sarah Ellender had, and it worried her greatly. Eliza stopped and said a quick prayer.

The death of its mate, so close to Sarah and Samuel's cabin, was not a good sign at all. But Eliza felt it was best to not mention the incident to Sarah Ellender. Eliza thought, "No sense borrowing trouble." So, she kept it to herself, but it worried her for a long time to come.

Samuel dug up two large sweet bubbie plants and planted them under the windows of the cabin. He had spotted the plants one day as he crossed over the ridge to check on the apple trees he had planted. He told Sarah Ellender, "When summer rolls around, you will have the scent of sweet bubbies coming straight in through the windows. Sweet bubbies for my sweet wife," he said with a smile.

He treated Sarah Ellender better than anyone else could have. She grew to love him even more with each passing year.

It was nearly two years before Sarah Ellender was with child. Little Mariah was born in September, about the time that the bead bush trees began to drop their leaves along Big Rock Creek. Samuel was so proud of his little daughter. Sarah Ellender watched him as he held Mariah for the first time, wrapped tightly in a blanket that Sarah Ellender had made while tears of joy rolled down his face.

"My darling Samuel," Sarah Ellender said as she choked back her own tears. "What a tenderhearted man I married, a man with a heart of gold. I chose well for myself." She smiled as her tears fell in earnest. Samuel kissed her and said gently, "I'm the one who did the choosing, but the good Lord sure helped me do it."

Little Mariah was an inquisitive toddler and was constantly seeking to learn more about the world around her. Sarah Ellender had already begun teaching her how to identify the healing plants that grew in the area, and which illnesses were helped by the medicinal herbs. Mariah was a quick study, just like her mother. As soon as she could talk, she was able to name the plants as well as Sarah Ellender herself.

One day, she was off and running through the high grass and happily pointing out each plant, singing out its name to her mother. She ran farther away than Sarah Ellender liked, so she got up from the blanket she had spread out in the grassy field and called out to Mariah. When the laughing toddler abruptly sat down in the grass, Sarah Ellender was able to catch up with her. That was when she heard it—the distinctive rattle of a snake, somewhere between her and little Mariah. She figured by the sound that it was somewhere in the three feet of space between them, hidden from view in the grass. Sarah Ellender stood rigid, frozen in fear.

Suddenly, the snake slithered out of the grass directly toward Mariah. The markings on the snake were distinctive: a pinkish color and the unmistakable band of brown that ran the length of its back. Sarah Ellender recognized it instantly. It was a timber rattler, poisonous and very deadly. She was nearly mindless with terror.

Little Mariah laughed as she watched a butterfly flutter from one tiny field flower to the next, totally unaware of the danger lurking so close to her. Sarah Ellender could hardly breathe. She began to pray. She prayed as she had never prayed before. The snake slid closer to the baby's leg, and it raised its head, tongue slithering. Then its thick body slid over the baby's ankle and across her leg. The seconds ticked off slowly, and Sarah Ellender watched, too terrified to make even the slightest move, afraid she would startle the snake and cause it to strike. With everything in her, she willed herself to remain still, except for her lips as she feverishly prayed. Perspiration beads formed quickly on her upper lip as she continued to pray silently.

"Please, dear Lord, place your angels beside my baby girl. Don't let this snake take my baby here, in this field of flowers and sunshine. Please, precious Lord and Father, hear my prayer!"

Sarah Ellender shuddered at the sight of her baby girl's leg being rubbed with the large snake's body. It slithered over her foot, and Mariah kicked lightly, still laughing, and the snake slowly slid off and away into the grass. In that instant, Sarah Ellender grabbed Mariah up, gathering her close to her chest and ran with all her might, out of the field. She went flying toward the cabin. Mariah giggled as she jostled about in her mother's arms. Sobbing and thanking the Lord, Sarah Ellender held little Mariah close to her and kissed every inch of her soft, plump baby limbs. *God is good*, thought a grateful Sarah Ellender, *God is so good!* She let out a long breath and sank to her knees.

Little Mariah squealed out in her baby speak an excited, "God is good!" It was almost as if the baby had somehow heard her mother's very thoughts. Sarah Ellender hung her head and sobbed in relief.

Jane held the handwritten pages close to her chest as she sighed in relief. *God is good*, she thought with tears in her eyes. She was amazed at how well Isabelle could tell a story. She could make you feel as if you were right there at the moment as it was happening.

She sipped her coffee and then grimaced as she realized it had gone completely cold. She set down the cup and kept right on reading.

Not long after the snake incident, Sarah Ellender found out she was pregnant once more. This time, a baby boy was born, and as Samuel liked to say, "A little fellow came along to live with our family, right there in the cabin." The boy that came to live with them was called

Welzia Augustus. Samuel was thrilled to have a son; it was a dream of his come true.

When Welzia was old enough to toddle, he went with Sarah Ellender to check on her bees. She was well known in the area for her honey. She kept her bees in gums or hollow logs. The bee gum got its name from the black gum tree, but Sarah Ellender had discovered that honey bees loved cedar gums, so she began making hers out of cedar.

The art of bee hunting and beekeeping was an old one, handed down with each generation. They would first go out into the woods and observe the bees. They would closely watch them as they went from their water source and back to their hive, which would give away the location of the hive. The bees usually got water from mossy or sandy areas, such as around a creek bed, and they would fly basically in a straight line back to their hive.

It took keen eyesight to be able to follow the flight of the bees. Sarah Ellender knew that the best time to hunt for bees was when the apple trees were blooming, so when it was time, they went out to search. Welzia also soon learned to watch for signs of honeydew, which was the secretion that insects left after eating the plants. They left this honeydew in droplets on the leaves. This secretion is gathered up by the bees and the honey produced by it is a rich, dark color, highly prized for its medicinal properties.

The signs the mountain offered were continually read by the residents and heeded accordingly. The wooly worm predicted the weather by its color bands, if over one-third of the worm's marking was dark colored, that usually signaled an early winter. What time the wooly worms traveled, to weave the web that would be their winter home, also gave clues as to what the weather would be like that coming winter.

Welzia quickly learned the art of beekeeping, using medicinal plants and herbs, and watching for weather signs from his mother—and the ways of farming and preaching from his father. His lessons were learned quickly, as he was a decidedly intelligent young boy.

Samuel loved little Welzia, and he saw in him the same potential that his own father had seen in his son. Welzia also had the same quiet demeanor that his father possessed. He was a mixture of Sarah Ellender and his father, and he made them both very proud.

17

We should be astonished at the goodness of God, stunned that He should bother to call us by name, our mouths wide open at His love, bewildered that at this very moment we are standing on holy ground.

~Brennan Manning

Welzia began to preach at an early age, as did most of the preachers in his family. He knew what he was destined to be, and never wavered far from the path that had been chosen for him.

Welzia was called to the deathbed of an elderly woman who belonged to the church while his father was away on the circuit preaching. He was just a lad of twelve, but being the son of a preacher, he knew how to pray, and pray well.

Welzia entered the house quietly and walked respectfully up to the bed, where the elderly lady lay.

Her daughter, distraught and crying, sat in the corner of the room.

Welzia strode confidently closer to the woman and in the best imitation of his father that he could summon, he delivered a soulful, earnest prayer. He reached out and took her hand. At the end of his prayer, he reverently sang the words of an old hymn. His sweet tenor voice rang out strong and sure in the room.

Martha Arrowood Pelc

"On Hallelujah Avenue, I'll have a mansion fine,
Where the tree of life is blooming,
God's love will always shine.
No death will ever enter, no troubles, cares, or woe.
I'll have a million years in glory
with a million more to go."

The daughter wiped her eyes and sang the last line of the song along with Welzia. Welzia walked out of the house and started toward home after the lady had passed through the gates of heaven to be with her Lord.

Welzia was never the same after that. He knew without a doubt that his life would be spent serving the Lord, in every way that he could. He saw how the simple act of caring had touched the heart of the dying lady's daughter. She was in great need, and something as simple as even the prayer from a child had soothed her. God had worked a miracle through Welzia. Welzia understood this completely.

Welzia came upon an old fallen tree trunk along the pathway home, and crying hard with his shoulders heaving, the boy knelt down in the thick grass beside the old log and prayed. He clasped his hands together and bowed his head. He asked God for strength, especially for when his voice felt so small, and he asked God to guide him from that day forward along the path he was to take.

And Welzia knew, without a doubt, that his prayers had been heard.

Old Lady Schnitzler

The wind was blowing hard. It was early autumn, and the leaves blew across the dirt road ahead of them, like crabs skittering about on a sandy beach. One boy in the group absently kicked at a rock, and when it clattered loudly, they all flinched at the sound. A quiet

Love and Mercy - Up On Roan Mountain

hush had fallen over the mountain, as the sky slowly darkened into a purple bruised color, and the only sound was the wind blowing through the dried leaves that night.

Welzia, being the smallest and youngest boy, had hung back in the group with the girls, Patty, and Annette. Little Patty and Annette were two sweet sisters who lived nearby, who often came to the creek near the cabin to play with Welzia.

Welzia guessed that most all kids liked to play around a creek. His father had warned him about damming the creek up, but Welzia guessed all kids liked to do that, too. They had dammed the creek up just last week and made themselves a jim-dandy swimming hole.

It was the same cold and clear water that usually came down from the mountain, but the swimming hole had turned the water dark and murky real fast. Anyway, the creek pushed through the dam with the first hard rain. The rain soon washed clear away all the signs that it was ever even there. So Welzia figured it didn't hurt much to dam it up. Welzia listened to his folks, for the most part, and he felt guilty for disobeying.

He knew he shouldn't be going over to the next holler after being told not to. But still, down the road he went with the rest of the group. All the others were giggling and whispering among themselves, but Welzia walked with his head hung low. It hung almost as low as he felt on the inside that night. He knew that Samuel would wear him out, good and proper, when he did find out about him coming here. But as it turned out, Samuel never did.

Up ahead, some distance off the dirt road, a light was shining through the trees. It was shining from the window of Old Lady Schnitzler's house. She was really old, Welzia thought. Welzia figured her to be about a hundred and twenty years old, at least, maybe older.

She had been widowed for a long time now. She had come over straight from Germany, or at least that's what most people in the area thought. She came over the ocean on a big boat, and her folks mostly stayed behind, back in Germany. She talked real funny, with her accent, and she didn't sound like anyone else Welzia had ever heard. The townsfolk all thought she was strange. So the kids felt the same way, as kids tend to do. *Whatever the grown-ups think, well, when you're a kid, you think it's just naturally the right thing*, Welzia thought logically.

Old Lady Schnitzler had told stories that had the mountain women all upset. Welzia had overheard the women talking about it when they were all sitting on the porch shelling peas and snapping half-runner green beans. Women talked a lot, Welzia had often observed. *But you can sure learn a lot if you just listen to them.*

He didn't think it was a sin to listen if they were just talking right out loud, sitting right there on the porch. They weren't whispering or covering their mouths or anything like that; they were just talking normally. No one had ever told him that you couldn't just listen, anyway.

The women seemed pretty scared of old Mrs. Schnitzler. She'd had three husbands, and they all had died one right after another. Now that wasn't so strange, not really. Welzia knew that people got sick, and sometimes they died. But Mrs. Schnitzler had known each and every time that they were *going* to die. She knew even if they were going about their business just like they always had, and they were not sick or acting sick or anything. That was the part that wasn't normal, and it really spooked the women. Most wouldn't say anything about it at church, but they sure would talk about it on someone's porch, or at the kitchen table.

"Well, one thing for sure, she's not from around here. She talks using such strange-sounding words. Words you have never heard in all your life," said Mary Jane Holtsclaw matter-of-factly. "She speaks in her German tongue, and she stands there with her hand up on her hip, and she just dishes it out of the bucket with her other hand."

She put one hand on her hip to demonstrate. Several ladies giggled at this. Welzia guessed she was meaning she used her hands when she talked, gesturing. "She pulls that hay right out of a bale and hands it right over to you, time after time. The whole time she talks, she does it. You have never seen the likes of it in all your livelong days, I tell you," Mary Jane said, chuckling.

"Well, I ain't so worried about how she talks, as I am about what she says," Esther May said. She pursed her lips up funny. "Sort of like a baby who had eaten something that tasted real bad and just didn't like it at all," Welzia thought to himself.

Then she looked at the other ladies, slyly, out of the corners of her eyes. "It just ain't normal, that's what it is."

The rest of the women murmured in agreement as their hands and fingers kept working, nonstop. They hardly ever look down at their hands while they work. And it never ceased to amaze Welzia how they were able to do that.

He slid around the kitchen door, just another inch or so closer, keeping his head close to the door so he could better hear what they were saying.

"She claims she heard a watch just a ticking away that last time her husband passed. A death watch, she was a-calling it," Esther Faye said.

"Well, I just hope to never," Leota Furn said.

"Me, neither," said another. A few more unsettled murmurings came from the women.

"Now, what in land's sake is a dadgum 'death watch,' anyways?" Ruth Bewley asked.

"Why, she claimed she heard it a-ticking, just like a watch. She went all about and done searched the whole house over, three times, even went on down to the cellar, trying to find where the watch was. It just kept right on a-ticking," Esther May said. "But whenever she thought she had gotten close to the sound, the ticking would just up and move away."

"She said it would just up and move away?" Ruth Bewley asked in a high voice with raised eyebrows.

"Why, it sure would. It would just start right back up to ticking, somewhere else in the house," said an almost breathless Mary Jane.

Welzia sucked in his breath with wide eyes. "It was just a-ticking like a watch, like it was ticking off the minutes until someone was dead," said another lady in the group.

Stiff and dead like the squirrel I found in the woods and poked with that stick, Welzia thought. *Stiff and hard. Stone dead.* Welzia shuddered.

The death watch had come three times to the home of Mrs. Schnitzler. Each time it had come, the husband she was married to at the time had never once heard the ticking. Everyone else in the house had surely heard it, and it drove them all crazy. But not the poor soul that death was a-coming for, they never hear a thing. Death always seemed to have a way of letting some people know its coming. Mrs. Schnitzler was certainly sure of that. She had laid out the clothes that he was to be buried in, the third time she heard the ticking. She accepted what it meant, just like you accept that dark clouds in a summertime sky, along with that unmistakable metallic smell in the air, will eventually bring on the rain.

Mrs. Schnitzler had stopped talking about it after a while, but the ladies sure hadn't. Something about it made them all plenty upset. Welzia thought it was a good thing to know when someone was fixing to up and die, just so's you could be ready and all. He sure hoped that whenever death came back to the mountain, he could hear that ticking just plain as day and that all his family could hear it, too.

Mrs. Schnitzler knew a lot of things that his momma said she just shouldn't. But somehow, she just naturally knew. Welzia wondered why she knew those things, but he guessed some people were, well, just different. Welzia thought that maybe God figured that some people needed to know things, and maybe He gave them this "sight" as a gift. Whatever the reason, he thought it was terribly interesting.

Sarah Ellender suddenly spoke in a low voice, right into his ear. She was standing just inches behind Welzia. "Now, you just go on outside now and find something to entertain yourself with. I will be out there to talk to you, directly."

She placed a hand on his shoulder firmly and gave a slight push for emphasis. Welzia's shoulders slumped under her touch. He instinctively knew that he was in trouble.

She must have seen me skulking here, behind the door like I was listening in on them ladies a-talking, Welzia thought, deflated. *Even if I wasn't up to nuthin' much at all, it sure looked like I was. Skulking around is something that mommas just don't like. And they just never will.*

With downcast eyes and his hands jammed into his pockets, he touched the door facing with the toe of his shoe, out of habit and headed outside, downhearted.

Later on that evening, as he walked with the others toward the Schnitzler house, with the darkening skies closing in, he wasn't afraid—well, not really. But he wasn't about to let anyone think that he was, either. He was really just wondering. Mostly he was wondering about what it was they were all gonna do when they got there. There wasn't any real plan. That was the worst part, the not knowing what to expect part.

The lights were out in the house. Welzia thought it was odd. He knew he had seen a light shining before, but he did not think too much about it. The small group of kids whispered among themselves, and they huddled tighter together as they made their way up the path to the front door. They quietly stepped onto the porch, and two stayed at the top step while the rest went over to the front windows.

Annette was peering in the window, and Patty whispered breathlessly from beside Welzia, "Can you see anythin' at all?" Annette shook her head and pushed her nose up against the pane, cupping her hands around her eyes, trying to see. It was dark inside. Way too dark. Then Danny and Isaac jumped off the end of the porch, into the lilac bushes at the side of the house. Welzia still stood at the front door steps, standing real still.

Welzia had no sooner thought to himself that something sort of felt odd when a deafeningly loud screech shattered the silence, followed quickly by yet another one. The first ear piercing screech had come from just above where Danny and Isaac had landed, under the tree branch.

All the hair on Welzia's head stood up at once, and it felt like each one was waving at the other. Pure pandemonium ensued.

Welzia was nearly run over by Patty, who fled the scene without even a second's pause. Welzia felt the breeze as she blew on past him. Annette jumped clean off the porch, missing the steps entirely, and was a blur in just the blink of an eye, her curls bobbing up and down while flying out behind her. Danny knocked Isaac back into the lilac bushes in his haste to get up, and he ran right off into the darkness. Isaac clambered to his feet and tore off in the direction of his house, never slowing down to look back once, panic-stricken.

Welzia figured it had to have been Isaac, by far the worst scaredy-cat of the group, who had screamed out in sheer terror. Poor old Isaac had hit an even higher note than that old screech owl ever had. Welzia, coming to his senses, turned to flee and with a sudden wallop, he was stopped by a solid wall. It was a wall that had suddenly appeared on the walkway, just below the steps, in the darkening light.

When he scrambled onto his knees and looked up, there she was. Old Lady Schnitzler. She was the "wall" he had slammed smackdab into. She just stood there, wide and stout, built solid and sturdy, like an old oak tree that would not even flinch if a locomotive hit it, full on. She scowled down at Welzia and as he looked up at her, then past her, he could just make out the girls' white petticoats flashing up in the darkness as they ran across the meadow. Everyone had flown the coop, and here he was left on his own. This didn't look good for him at all. Welzia knew by her stance that Old Lady Schnitzler meant business this time. Her hands were planted firmly on her ample waist.

She bellowed out, *"Kommen Sie mit?"* Of course, Welzia had not a clue as to what that meant. But he got the gist of the meaning soon enough. She grabbed him up by a fistful of his collar and nearly dragged him up the stairs and into the front door. The dim moonlight was the only light falling into the house, through the glass in the front room. She moved silently in the darkness, and Welzia just stood there, shaking in his shoes.

Old Lady Schnitzler had known. She had known we were coming, way before we got here, and she had put out the kerosene lamps so that we could not see in. She does know when things are gonna happen. She probably eats boys like me for her supper, Welzia thought in a rapid flow. He instantly began praying in earnest. His lips were moving feverishly in the dark room. He wasn't so sure God would see fit to help him now since he had come here after being told not to. But he figured it couldn't hurt, not one bit, to pray, and pray hard. So Welzia prayed.

She lit the lamps, one by one, and the room soon glowed brightly. The light glinted off the pretty glassware that sat on the side table. Pretty, intricately colored glass, like none Welzia had ever seen before. *That must be real genuine German glass*, Welzia thought. *Pretty-colored German glass is gonna be the last thing I see before I die.* He gulped. His eyes were as big as saucers.

Mrs. Schnitzler went into the kitchen and made some noise. It sounded to Welzia like the cabinets were opening and closing, and the dishes were rattling. Welzia figured she was getting ready to make him up into a stew or something. His legs were shaking so bad that he couldn't move from the spot where he stood, couldn't even run away. *Betrayed by my very own legs. I sure never saw this a-coming*, he thought.

Old Lady Schnitzler appeared in the doorway and the shadows from the lamplight danced across her face. The shadows contorted her features, making her seem even more menacing. Welzia closed his eyes tight, not wanting to see what she had planned for him next. Welzia could hear the floorboards creaking under her weight as she moved closer to him. He peeked up at her, and when she had made her way over to where he was standing, she extended her hand out toward him.

Welzia leaned back away from her hand and kept his eyes locked on her face. Her eyes glittered in the lamp's glow.

Then he glanced down.

She was offering him some cookies on a painted dish. He looked again at the cookies and then at her face, and a smile appeared as her scowl left. Welzia could not believe it. She was smiling at him. Welzia stared at her for a moment, and then he swallowed hard and slowly smiled back.

Turns out that Old Lady Schnitzler was not the evil woman that all the other women thought she was, after all. She was just a lonely old lady who made awfully good cookies. And, oh yes, she did know things. She knew all sorts of things. She did eventually make that stew that Welzia thought she was making, but she made it with chicken, and it didn't have even one little boy in it. She called it "slumgullion," which Welzia figured meant *stew* in German. It was very good stew, too.

Later that week, while lying on his back in the grassy field and giving it some thought, Welzia decided that sometimes people do know things. And it's not their fault if they can see things that are a-coming. It's not their fault at all. It may even be a divine gift straight from God.

Welzia had left Old Lady Schnitzler's later that evening with a fistful of her delicious cookies. Welzia eventually convinced the others into coming back with him, to visit her. He told them that Mrs. Schnitzler liked to talk, and she talked a lot. But, boy howdy, you really can learn a lot if you just listen.

The next two children born to Sarah Ellender and Samuel were William Morgan and Samuel, Jr. William was a thoughtful, brooding child, and Samuel, Jr. was happy and fun loving. Welzia, being the older brother, looked out for his siblings as best he could. After Samuel, Jr. came Eliza Caroline, almost three years later. Then, after another six years, John Henry was the little boy who came to live with them. Samuel knew in his heart that John Henry would be another minister as well. Turns out he was right. But, sadly, Samuel never got to see it.

The dead turtle did serve as an omen, just as it was predicted. Samuel took ill suddenly and took to his bed. He seemed just fine one morning but by that afternoon he was quite ill. Sarah Ellender tried every remedy she knew, but nothing seemed to help him. He just kept getting worse and worse. His appendix had ruptured, but Sarah Ellender had no way of knowing.

She summoned a doctor from Johnson City over in Washington County, but by the time he made it over the mountain, Samuel did not have much time left. Sarah Ellender prayed to God, asking Him not to take Samuel from her. She prayed that God wouldn't let Samuel suffer terribly. It was the hardest thing Sarah Ellender ever had to do, to just stand beside him and watch, and not be able to help him. Her attempts to comfort Samuel had seemed so heartbreakingly futile.

What would she do, all alone, with six children and all of them under the age of fourteen? But God thought it was best, and He called Samuel home at the young age of thirty-six. She held his hand tightly as his life slowly ebbed away, breaking poor Sarah Ellender's heart. She was devastated.

Life became hard for Sarah Ellender. She eventually returned to live with her Winters family up on the Doll Flats. But they had it difficult enough themselves, with five teenagers of their own, and she felt it was unfair to bring her family into the household to feed, as well. She worked hard to try and keep the wolf from the door.

She was a midwife, sold her honey and did anything she could to support her family and keep them all together. Then, in July of the same year that Samuel died, Sarah Ellender remarried. Dave Miller was eighteen years older than Sarah Ellender and had lost his wife some three years prior. Dave also had seven children to raise without a partner, so they married and blended the two families together. Dave had been crippled in the war, but he did the best he could to provide for the family.

After Sarah Ellender and Dave had married, they had five more children together.

The family had its share of ups and downs. The blending of two family units, under one roof, was never easy. They owned and operated a grist mill that provided a meager amount of income until a devastating flood washed it away.

The older boys of Samuel and Sarah Ellender soon made their own way, easing the burden off of their mother.

Dave was especially hard on her children, and he was happy to see the older boys out of the house and on their own.

So that's how Welzia came to be working as a hired hand on the Garland farm, where he first met Isabelle, Jane thought with a nod. She pulled her legs up underneath herself, to get more comfortable, and continued reading the last few pages of the old, tattered letters.

The years had moved stealthily on by, as time has a way of doing. After Dave Miller had passed away, Sarah Ellender went to live with Welzia and Isabelle.

Then, when Sarah Ellender died in 1914, they buried her in a tiny country church cemetery, in the family plot. She knew in her heart that she would never leave the mountain—she was born there, and that was where her heart remained.

Even after all those years, her free spirit still roams the Doll Flats, standing on her favorite ridge at sunset, watching the sun slowly fade away into rose-colored clouds in the summer sky. She has kept constant watch over that beloved ridge. In her heart, it was *her* mountain, after all, and it always would be.

18

God's promises are like the stars; the darker the night the brighter they shine.

~DAVID NICHOLAS

JANE WALKED STRAIGHT out of the house after reading the very last line of the final packet of tattered letters. She went quickly up the path to the hidden cemetery near the house. She located the exact spot, just as the letters had described, where David had been buried. He had lain right here, beneath these honeysuckle vines, in this grave with no marker, for all these years, forgotten. She knew in her heart exactly what she needed to do.

She called Pastor Bob McCully in Dallas, North Carolina, and asked him to come up the following weekend to officiate at the service. She knew that Pastor Bob would find just the perfect words to say. He was an eloquent speaker and a much-beloved minister to Jane. And, most importantly, Jane felt that he was the absolute perfect choice to perform a very special blessing of the grave, with the placing of the new marker. David was finally going to get a proper burial ceremony, after all, the proper Christian funeral that had long been denied him.

The following weekend, Pastor Bob's wife, Mimi, petite and dainty, and beautifully attired in a sundress with pretty flowers, attended the service with him. The family gathered out on the lawn and walked together up the path. Each held bouquets of wildflowers, tied up with white ribbons.

Pastor McCully gave a beautiful, heartfelt prayer, requesting that "Angels and light surround and keep watch over the sacred final resting place of David." "May he find peace in heaven, an absolute perfect peace, the peace that he never attained here on earth." "May he know that his family understands completely what happened, so very long ago."

"I want to read a passage now from the Holy Bible," Pastor McCully said in a steady voice that carried on the warm wind that blew off the mountain that day. "This passage is from the book of Luke, Chapter 12, verse 4: 'And I say unto you, my friends, be not afraid of them that kill the body, and after that have no more that they can do.'"

Pastor Bob paused for a moment and turned the pages of his Bible to the book of John, Chapter 15, verse 13. He then read aloud in a strong, sure voice:

"No greater love hath a man, that he lays down his life for a friend."

"No greater love had David, for he laid down his own life to save his wife, Nancy, whom he loved greatly."

Pastor McCully sang "Amazing Grace", solo. His melodious voice rang out beautifully under the canopy of trees and floated in the breeze across the ridge. After he had finished singing, he spoke again.

"David was not a murderer, and he was not a deserter. Nor was David a coward. We pray for his soul that entered into eternal rest so many years ago, with our Savior above. May angels surround you, always."

Everyone gathered around and in unison they sang the old song "Peace like a River," and afterward they each filed past and placed their flowers at the base of the marker for David.

Love and Mercy - Up On Roan Mountain

Jane felt such a wonderfully tranquil and soothing peace within her heart. She knew, without a doubt, that doing this was necessary. It was long overdue, and she felt this was the only way to somehow right the terrible wrong from so long ago. Jane had tears flowing down her cheeks, and as she looked around at her loved ones, she saw all their tears, and she realized they all felt the power that this gravesite blessing held for David.

Later that coming week, Jane wanted to go again and pay her respects to David, alone.

She walked to the edge of the woods and up the path with a large bouquet of fresh flowers tied up with a ribbon. She had wandered up on the ridge and picked them earlier that morning when the dew was still clinging to the grass. She smelled their sweet smell and thought about the morning's red-and-golden sunrise, and how beautiful the springtime truly was on the mountain. She walked past the headstones she had found some months before, but now the brambles were all cleared away. The grass was mowed neatly. She had made sure all of the markers that had fallen had been repaired and placed upright. She walked over to the beautiful white marble marker, the one that she had just placed. The grass was coming in nicely where she had sown it, at the foot of the marker, all green and soft. She gently laid the bouquet of flowers down on the grave. She reached out and lightly traced her fingertip on the etching that read:

~ David Correll ~

Hung For A Murder
He Did Not Commit

~ Rest In Peace ~

And there, etched at the base of the marker, was a rosebud with the inscription, "Forever Loved."

Jane bent down and laid her hand on the marker, saying a silent prayer. Then, after a while, she turned and walked back toward the house. As she came into the clearing, she looked at the house, and her heart smiled. Home again. It was just beautiful. The flowers along the walkway were in full bloom. The bright yellow buttercups were nodding their heads in the light breeze.

The old sagging porch was replaced, and new shutters adorned the gleaming windows. The house was back, and in her full glory once again. The air was laden with the smell of spring and Jane felt content.

Later that night, asleep in her bed, Jane dreamed again. Or was she dreaming at all? She saw a light coming down the hallway. The light's glow illuminated the doorway of her room, and suddenly, in walked Welzia. Jane sat up in the bed, amazed.

Surely, I am still dreaming, she thought. Welzia was still the young boy who had just been to see Old Lady Schnitzler. He smiled tentatively at her and toed his boot against the bedpost and curled his arms around it, and then shyly looked at his feet. Then, into the room walked Samuel. He was so handsome and wide shouldered, even taller than she had imagined him to be. He walked over to Welzia and smiled at him and tousled his dark hair. Samuel held his Bible in his right hand, and he smiled a smile of pure gratitude to Jane, and she smiled back, nodding with understanding. Welzia took Samuel's hand, and they turned and left the room together. Welzia turned back and smiled at Jane, and with a small wave, he was gone.

Isabelle then came into the room with Mary Calla. Isabelle was once again the young girl who had cared for Mary Calla, about the age that she had been when she married Welzia. She was holding hands with her beautiful younger sister. They were both bathed in iridescent light, and Jane smiled when she saw how happy they looked. They smiled back at her and nodded, knowingly. Jane nodded her head in return. Isabelle turned as if someone had called out to her, in the direction of the hallway. She gave Jane another nod and a smile. She was thanking Jane, and Jane somehow knew how much it meant to Isabelle to be able to right this wrong.

Her family, once broken, was now complete again.

Sarah Ellender came in next, the lady in the mirror. Only this time, she was younger and very beautiful. Her long hair was loose and flowing, just like it was on the day of the church gathering. She still had a few apple blossoms stuck in her hair. She smiled at Jane, and reached out and took her hand. Jane nodded that she understood completely, and as she watched Sarah Ellender closely, a single tear formed and rolled down Sarah Ellender's cheek.

Jane wanted to ask Sarah Ellender so many things. She wanted to truly know this wonderful woman, but just as Jane started to speak, Sarah Ellender put her finger to her lips, smiled, and then she was gone.

Jane looked around the room, startled, but they were all gone, just like that.

Then the light in the hallway reappeared and in walked Nancy and David, hand in hand.

Nancy was smiling, but a stream of tears coursed down her cheeks. They were young, the age when their life together was forever shattered. David reached out and laid his hand upon Jane's as it lay on the bed. Instantly she felt his raw emotions. She knew he was trying to thank her. Many words passed between them without one ever being spoken aloud. She took his hand, and they stayed hand in hand for a moment longer. Nancy reached out and took Jane's other hand. Flashes of the agony this couple had endured flew through Jane's mind, and she understood completely what it had been like for them. They smiled again, and the understanding needed no words.

David and Nancy then turned toward the door, and Nancy turned back to Jane for one last look and in a bright flash of light, they left. Jane shielded her eyes from the dazzling white light, and when she lowered her hand, the room was empty.

Jane sat there on the bed, barely breathing. Her mind was racing. *Yes, of course, I was dreaming. This time I'm sure—no, positive. I'm positive it was just a dream.*

Sometimes you really can learn a lot if you just listen, Jane thought to herself with a smile. The smile lingered on her face, and she sat there a moment and pondered it all. She took a deep breath and then she pushed back the covers and got up out of bed to make herself some coffee.

19

There's something like a line of gold thread running through a man's words when he talks to his daughter, and gradually over the years it gets to be long enough for you to pick up in your hands and weave into a cloth that feels like love itself.

~John Gregory Brown

Jake was coming to get her today. He was going to take her to the rhododendron festival that was in full swing over at the state park.

She was busy making herself presentable. She dabbed a bit of her best perfume behind her ears, feeling especially festive today. She and Jake had been seeing each other just about every day now, and she felt that the relationship was going somewhere this time. For the first time in a long while, she let herself hope so, anyway. *Take it just one day at a time, now, girlie*, she cautioned herself. She knew that things could turn on a dime. If anyone knew this, she sure did.

The house had seemed almost to sigh in satisfaction when the renovations were finally completed. She knew in her heart that staying put was exactly what she should have done, instead of going elsewhere. She belonged here now, and this house surely belonged to her. *Well, maybe it belongs to both of us, or will eventually*, she thought with a lingering smile.

Later, after she had dressed and tidied up the bathroom, she walked through the hall and into the kitchen to get a drink of water. Jane stopped suddenly in her tracks in the doorway of the kitchen and backed up a step into the hall. She turned and caught a second glimpse of two little girls, skipping, hand in hand, down the hall and into the great room.

The smaller of the two girls turned around and smiled at Jane. Her long hair hung in a thick braid behind her back. Jane knew instantly that this little girl just had to be Minnie. While smiling back at her and slowly shaking her head, she said to herself, *You have totally lost it, girl.* Jane purposely chose not to let this incident cloud the day's events, so she just put it aside, for now.

The festival was amazing. The colors on the mountain were simply breathtaking. The blaze of pink and fuchsia from the laurel seemed to go on for miles. The hazy blue horizon off in the distance combined with the indescribable green of the meadow was something else to see.

The mountaintop was packed with sightseers. The seasonal influx of people caused the tiny community's population to swell each and every summer significantly. It was a boost to the local economy, but traffic was a bear.

After they saw everything they could and looked at all the crafts for sale, then sampled most of the food from the vendors, they decided to call it a day.

Jane had taken tons of pictures with her camera and just knew she had nabbed "the shot," the one that was just perfect, of the mountain laurel in a blaze of color. It was the one that she knew she would frame and hang over the mantel.

The picture would be the last piece of decoration placed in her perfect home on the mountain.

Jake carried her backpack and camera gear back to the truck and helped her up into the seat. Once seated, she expected him to hand her the gear. She turned to grab it, and he offered her up a small black box instead. Jane's breath caught in her throat when she realized what it had to be, tucked inside that tiny box.

Not just a ring, it was *the* ring. A perfect, heart-shaped diamond was inside. Jane stared at it in total disbelief. She knew that he would have never offered her a ring unless he was totally serious about marrying her. He knew how badly she had been hurt in the past, and she had told him that it would have to be perfect between them, beyond any shadow of a doubt, before she would ever commit again. She was pretty sure that what they had, was as close to perfect as it gets.

Jake smiled at her and said, "Make me the happiest man on the mountain, and say yes." Jane just sat there not saying anything, staring at him. Jake couldn't stand it any longer. He slowly lowered the hand that held the box. His face showed the intense hurt he was feeling.

She stammered, "I'm just saying let's make sure. I'm not saying no."

Jake spoke hardly a word as they drove back to the house on the Doll Flats. She looked out the window and then at her camera gear, anywhere but in his direction. She knew she had hurt him. But she could not just come right out and say yes when her heart was saying *hold on now, just wait a minute*. It was so wonderful, just knowing that he wanted to marry her, but at the same time, it was so terrifying.

She thought of how badly her heart had been broken before, and she sure didn't want a repeat of that. She couldn't stand it. Her heart was just not up for yet another ugly breakup.

Two weeks passed, and there was still no word from Jake. She had cried it all out, finally. Eventually, she had decided that it was all for the best. It was just not meant to be, and that's the reason she had hesitated. She was certain of it now.

"A heart wants what it wants, and mine, evidently, wants just to stay single and safe." She sighed and quietly determined that it was time just 'to accept it and move on', whatever that meant.

I will be single from here on out, and just die alone, a miserable, bitter old scowling woman, she thought ruefully. She felt defeated and sad, but she accepted it.

She had gone out and bought new curtains for the upstairs bedroom, trying to pick up her spirits by adding a splash of color. She climbed the ladder and began installing the new curtain rods in the bedroom where the trunk sat.

She pounded in the nails and with each blow she made, she told herself over and over that she had done the right thing. *You need just to forget about that man. He's long gone by now, girlie.* But it made her heart even sadder, still.

She stepped down off the ladder and backed away to take a look at the rods, trying to determine if they were level. When she took yet another step backward, she bumped into the trunk and sat abruptly down on it, breaking her fall. "What in the world?" she asked the room. The trunk had been pushed back against the wall completely, yet no one had been up here but her. She knew she hadn't moved it out into the middle of the floor. It was certainly not there when she had entered the room—she would have surely noticed.

Jane sat there and puzzled over it. *There has to be something else that I need to know. Someone is trying to tell me something, again.* She sat in the silence and waited.

After a few moments, nothing happened, nothing at all. Feeling sort of silly, she stood up, turned around, and stared down at the trunk.

It just sat there. So she cautiously lifted the lid. Not knowing what to expect, she lowered her head and peeked into the small opening, holding up the top of the trunk only about six inches or so. Nothing flew out, and there were no strange lights, so she went ahead and opened it up all the way.

Inside, the bundles of letters were stacked neatly, just as she had placed them after she had read them, one after another. The ribbons were still neatly tied, and everything appeared to be just the same as she had left it. She sorted through the stacks and counted the journals, and everything was there. She reached up to pull the lid down to close it, and as she did, the corner of the lining fell. There had been a pearl brooch pinning the lining into place, but now the brooch was nowhere in sight.

Intrigued, Jane wiggled her fingers up under the edge of the material, working it loose, just enough to get her fingers further behind the cloth. There had been daisies printed on the lining at one time, but they had long since faded. Now, you could hardly make out the faint outline.

Her hand slid along the lid's curve, feeling for anything she may have missed, hidden there. Suddenly, she felt something.

There hadn't been anything there the first time she had looked; she was certain of it. But there was something there now.

It was an envelope with some weight to it. Something was folded up and placed within it. She turned it over, looking for markings, but she found none. Nothing, except for a name: "Jane" written on the front, printed out in block letters. She immediately recognized her father's handwriting. It was without a doubt, his same slanted "*J*".

Jane clutched the envelope to her chest as tears welled up in her eyes. Her hand trembled with emotion.

Oh, Daddy. I just knew if you could, you would let me know something. Oh, Dad, I just knew it. She sat down on the bed and pulled her legs up and sat crossed-legged. She could not bring herself to open this quickly; it needed to be done slowly and savored. She sat there, with tears streaming down her face for quite a while, while she turned the envelope over and over again in her hands. Her finger traced the letters of her name several times.

He knew she would inherit the house, of course, but he did not know she would want to restore it and move here. Or had he known what she would do all along?

What if she hadn't come up here at all and had just sold the house immediately? But her dad had known his daughter. He knew that it would be too precious to sell because he loved this house, and he loved the Roan. And she was his daughter.

She carefully opened the sealed envelope and sat, staring at it, for a few moments more, before reaching in and pulling out the pages that were neatly folded and tucked inside.

Seeing his handwriting again caused a fresh torrent of tears to flow.

The letter began, "My dear daughter," and Jane reached down to hold the hem of her T-shirt and dab the corners of her eyes before she could see to read the words.

If you are reading this letter, I have gone on to be with the others, and you have decided to keep the house. I am so glad that you have, Jane. I am so proud of who you have become. This mountain is in your blood, and life will be better for you here.

I know heartache has seemed to follow you, and it pained me greatly to see you hurting. When you were small, I could kiss your hurts away and make everything all better. But when you grew up, and I couldn't do that any longer, it sure broke your old dad's heart.

You will do fine, and life will get better for you, I just know it. Take those risks that may come your way, and grab life by the horns, girlie. Remember never to doubt yourself. Life passes way too quick to hesitate, even for a second. You won't regret any of the mistakes that you make, but you will regret all the risks you don't take.

Enjoy your life, and enjoy the beautiful sunsets over the mountain. Don't forget the sunrises, either. Remember who you are, and where you come from. Remember not to try and seek peace of mind from this world. You must seek God first. In finding Him, you will find all the peace your heart could ever desire. Stay true to yourself, and the rest will just naturally work out itself. We will meet back up, one day real soon. Your old dad promises you that. There's much more to come after this.

Look for me in the breeze that blows off the Roan, and I will be there, right beside you, always.

Love you, sweetheart
Dad

She smiled through a fresh bout of tears and took a lace hanky that her Aunt Ann had made for her, out of her jeans pocket and dabbed her eyes. *You have got to get a hold of this crying now*, she told herself. As she was thinking this, her head jerked up, suddenly in tune with her own special radar. She held her breath listening intently to the silence as she sat perfectly still. Then, she suddenly heard a noise coming from downstairs. The hair on the back of her neck stood up. She slowly tucked the letter into her shirt pocket and slid off the bed. She moved quickly over to the doorway and leaned in toward the door, listening intently.

Someone was definitely in the house. It sounded like someone was coming up the stairs. Each footfall was softly thudding in the silence of the house. She could hardly breathe. Panic took over, and she reached out for the curtain rod she had left standing against the wall and grabbed it up like a sword. The door creaked open, slowly.

And then a head appeared and turned slowly. Peering around the door was Jake.

Jane took a deep breath. It really was Jake. He smiled at her and said, "You know, I sure miss you when I don't get to see you."

She instantly dropped the curtain rod beside her, and it clanged loudly and then rolled and rattled away on the floor. She ran straight into his arms, flinging her arms around his neck and showering him with kisses.

"Yes. Yes. Yes! If the proposal still stands, I say yes!" Jake smiled widely as he picked her up and swung her around and then lifted her up high.

Laughingly, he said, "Looks like I've gotten myself into some serious trouble, girlie."

Jane nodded her head and then said, resignedly, "Oh, Mister, you have no idea."

Later that day, Jane walked into the great room to retrieve her purse, and there lying on the back of the chair where her purse sat, was an old white starched apron. Large pockets on the front of the apron were stitched in the finest lace crochet she had ever seen. As she held up the apron to get a closer look at the intricate detail, she noticed a name delicately embroidered into the edging: "Isabelle."

She stood staring in disbelief. All of the sorrows and suffering experienced down through the years in this family came flooding back to Jane in an instant. David freely giving his life for the woman he loved so desperately, and the anguish of the tremendous loss felt by his grieving widow. *This family has endured the pain and bitter torment of losing many of our beloved children, way before their time. With all the deaths and the losses, all of the heartaches and disappointments, and the many broken dreams that this family has suffered down through the generations, somehow we still find a way to go on. Our family survives, still. God has faithfully watched over each and every one of us, showing us His love and mercy, and continues to do so,* Jane thought.

This house still stands in testament of God's love. And will stand for years to come, and for the next generation to come, and the next, if I have anything at all to do with it. She lifted her chin in silent determination.

In one of the two large pockets on the front of the apron, there was a sizable lump. Jane realized that there must be something down in the pocket. She reached in, and first she pulled out a buckeye. Jane smiled. Then she pulled out an old pearl brooch. It was without a doubt the same one that had once held the lining of the trunk in place.

"So, you have decided to stay and see what happens next, have you, dear Grandma Isabelle?" Jane said aloud, her voice trembling with raw emotion. "Can't say that I blame you, can't blame you at all."

Jake walked into the room from the kitchen, where he had been oiling a squeaky cabinet hinge. "Did you say something just now, sweetheart?" Jake asked. Jane looked up, with her eyes brimming with tears and smiled at him.

Still holding the buckeye tightly in her hand, she said, "It was just the wind blowing through the pine trees again, whispering down to us from high up on the Roan."

Love and Mercy - Up On Roan Mountain

Poem written by:
Hilda Fay Arrowood Olive, May 17, 2015.

Mountain Tales and Memories

I love the old mountain stories, told to me by my precious dad.
Memories of bygone years were just about all the mountain people had.
Families were large back then, so they all worked hard all day.
You would not believe the games that they made up to play.

And you had it tough, growing up, says you.
Wasn't much play going on, with all those chores to do.
They raised their food and downed fowl and
animals with a single shot.
Times I ate at Great-Aunt Nora's there was
some good eatin' in the pot.
That woman could make the best apple butter that you ever ate.
All the food was scrumptious that was on my plate.

Remember the holy scripture about laying down your life?
Well, once a man confessed and was hung, protecting his wife.
Mountain folks are loyal and compassionate,
although sometimes described as slow.
I'm still very proud of my ancestors from
up on Roan Mountain's row.

There were sad times in "them thar hills,"
drownings, chokings, and flu.
People died so young, in spite of all that they could do.

Poor Grandma, no wonder my cousin said she was so mean,
Feeding that many kids on just a few potatoes and beans.
Hope she had a million fast cooking tricks.
It was hard enough for me, cooking just for six.

There is not enough praise for all those pioneers,
Who had mountain beauty to look at all through the years.
Oh please, don't cover up or destroy any more of that beautiful place.
If, by chance, God lets me make one more trip, I want to look for my family's place.

Epilogue

SOMETIMES YOU JUST have to tell your story and sometimes it takes you where you least expect it. There are a lot of actual truths written here, and they are mixed in with a generous helping of some "tall tales," as my dear dad used to say. But, there is certainly love in every line.

I've heard it said that you can choose your friends, but not your family. But, if given the choice, I believe I'd choose the very same family that God so generously blessed me with.

They were hard working and determined folk, and as my search for my roots continues, I am continually fascinated with the lives my ancestors lived. There is a speck of angel dust from our very own angels that went before us, hidden down deep, in each of us.

My father encouraged me to write and "get all the stories down on paper." I am saddened that I didn't complete this while he was still with us. But, something inside me tells me that he knows.

He already knows all about it.

My dear aunts, Ann, and Hilda, are to be commended for their tremendous support and enduring love of me. Especially when I had to be by far, the most annoying and aggravating of all their nieces. They helped me and encouraged me so much, I can't even begin to express my gratitude and love for them both.

A very special 'thank you' goes out to my cousin Tim-my newly found "brother", for providing me with heartfelt inspiration and especially for answering the call and continuing the Arrowood tradition of storytelling.

Thank you, Russ for always believing in me and cheering me on, every step of the way.

Without you, I'd be lost.
Probably lost somewhere up on a mountain, looking for another old cemetery.

Made in the USA
Columbia, SC
27 March 2019